G

this h
to no gud bastards

☆   ☆   ☆

The old man in the wagon nodded toward the corpse. "Should have left him hangin', son," he said.

"Why's that?"

"That's just the way it's supposed to be around here. Who are you, anyway?"

"Lex Cranshaw."

"Well, Mr. Cranshaw, looks like you bit yourself a mouthful of trouble. You better chew it fast and get on away from here."

"I'm here because of the hangings. I..."

"I seen the badge. But you got no business here. Ranger or not."

"What's your name? Who are you?"

"Jeremiah. You won't have no need of my last name. You won't be around long enough to use it."

"We'll see about that. You got a shovel in that wagon? Got to bury this man."

Jeremiah nodded slowly. "Better dig two holes while you're at it, Mr. Cranshaw."

★

THE RANGER

DAN MASON

HarperPaperbacks
A Division of HarperCollinsPublishers

This is a work of fiction. The characters, incidents, and
dialogues are products of the author's imagination and
are not to be construed as real. Any resemblance to actual
events or persons, living or dead, is entirely coincidental.

HarperPaperbacks *A Division of* HarperCollins*Publishers*
10 East 53rd Street, New York, N.Y. 10022

Cover art by Larry Schwinger

First HarperPaperbacks printing: December, 1990

Printed in the United States of America

HarperPaperbacks and colophon are trademarks of
HarperCollins*Publishers*

10 9 8 7 6 5 4 3 2 1

THE RANGER

1

E could see it from afar. It dangled like some strange fruit from the barren limb of a dead willow. It swayed in the hot wind sweeping across the high plains from New Mexico. As he rode closer, he was waiting for something to happen, for the dangling thing to disappear, maybe, or for it to climb up the thin filament attaching it to the tree, as if it were an oblong spider unable to spin a web.

But Lex Cranshaw knew that wasn't about to happen. It couldn't happen, and he knew it. That dark thing, just a blob on the end of a line, was why he was here. When he rode closer, he reined in, just a quarter mile away from it now. The thing was still indistinct, still swaying gently, like an old woman taking the air in a porch swing on a hot afternoon.

But he already knew what it was.

Reaching into his saddlebags, he wound the leather strap of his Confederate-issue binoculars in his thick fingers and jerked the glasses loose. He opened the leather pouch, pulled the glasses free and uncovered the lenses. He did it methodically, the way he did everything. He'd had the glasses for nearly ten years and there wasn't a scratch on the lenses. The sheepskin cover was long since worn to a soft, crumbly suede, but he didn't give a damn about that. They worked, and that's what mattered.

Bringing the field glasses close, he adjusted the focus with his thumb. He found the tree at once, the dangling thing took a little longer. He found the line, saw that it had been looped three times around a high branch and knotted tightly.

The noose was just as meticulously made. Six curls, the tag end of the line jutting just an inch above the thick coil that ended where the spine began. And the man on the end of the rope was stark evidence of just how well the rope had done its job. Cranshaw looped the binoculars around his neck, let them fall against his chest with a hollow thump, then spurred his big roan with a single poke of the rowels.

Cranshaw chewed at his lower lip as he rode closer. He watched the tall grass, noticed it bend under the breeze, and was glad he was upwind. Whoever it was on the end of the rope had been there awhile. He reined in fifty yards from the gently swaying corpse. Dismounting, he stood there, his fingers curled tightly around the reins.

The horse was skittish. It kept nickering and tossing its head, as if trying to convince him he'd already seen enough. But Cranshaw was stubborn. He let the reins fall and walked to the base of the tree. He put one hand on the trunk, as if afraid he might lose his balance, maybe get a little light-headed and fall over.

The dead man spun half a turn as the breeze kicked up for a few seconds. To Cranshaw, it looked almost like the way a man busy at a game of stud will turn to watch someone enter a saloon, never changing expression, never even blinking, then turn back to his cards. But the man on the end of the rope was long since through blinking. The eyes were long gone, pecked out by crows, probably. The putrid jelly oozing from the empty sockets looked about as inhuman as anything could. Just like the swollen black tongue sticking out of a corner of the mouth.

It was then Cranshaw noticed the ants. A steady stream of them, head to tail, down one side of the rope and up the other, pausing just long enough to pincer off a morsel and head home.

The smell was overpowering. This close, upwind was no protection. The corpse was actively asserting itself, demanding that one smell, even if he didn't care, or couldn't stand, to look.

Cranshaw let go of the tree and backed away a step, then started to circle. He saw one corner of a piece of paper, curled back toward the body. As he rounded the swaying body, he could see there was something scrawled on the paper. He pulled a kerchief from his pocket and stepped in closer.

this heres what happens to no gud bastards
The note had been printed with a pencil, a thick-leaded

one like carpenters use, he noticed. He was close enough
now to see the bugs swarming over the body and how
the clothing rippled not from the wind but from the teem-
ing insects beneath it. Cranshaw shook his head then circled back the way he'd come. At the base of the tree
he jumped, caught a low hanging limb, and hauled himself up.

Once in the tree, he moved out along the thick branch
until he could reach out and touch the rope. He felt the
scurry of ants, but held on, letting them crawl over his
knuckles as if they were no more than a momentary dis-
tortion of the rope. Cranshaw pulled a Bowie knife from
a sheath on his belt and sliced through the rope, pressing
the blade against the tree limb around which it had been
wound.

The cords severed with sharp pops and the last one
broke on its own. The body landed with a wet thud,
sounding more like a rotten melon than a thing of flesh
and bone. Putting the knife away again, he moved back
to the trunk, then slid down it with a grace unexpected
from so powerful a body.

Thomas Lexington Cranshaw, Lex for short, at least to
his friends, few as they were, had seen this kind of death
before. He'd seen it more often than he'd care to, in fact.
But death was everywhere these days, or so it seemed.
Almost like during the war, when he'd seen more than his
share of men, good and bad alike, too many young, and
near as many old, ground to pulp by ideas more powerful
than any machine, and all the more ruthless because they
were supposed to be ideals.

He'd been there when it was at its worst. He'd been young then, and more than a little foolish. But that was a more recent insight. With grape and minié balls flying, there had been no time for insight. There had only been time to take a breath and figure out how to live long enough to take another. But he had managed. He took one through the shoulder, and it might have saved his life, because it happened in a skirmish less than two hundred yards from Shiloh Church, thirty-six hours before the fighting really got out of control.

But what he'd seen had changed him somehow, made him harder, the way steel is tempered by a smith by constant pounding, heating, cooling, and heating again. He had become something other than what he had been. And that new something had played its own part in saving his life.

He remembered crawling through the weeds along a windbreak. He could see Union pickets not two hundred yards across a plowed field that had been rained on so hard and trampled so much its furrows were all gone, reduced to a thick skin of muddy clay. And when the sun came out, it baked the mud hard as stone, preserving for days, maybe weeks or even years, the footprints of hundreds of men.

The crack of muskets wouldn't let him sleep for long, and each time he woke up, he'd crawl until he could crawl no more. His eyes would close and he would drift away again, convinced he would never come back. What he remembered most, other than the pain which was so awful he wasn't sure he remembered it at all, was the sound of the flies as they followed him through the weeds, their angry buzzing filling his ears until he would wave one feeble hand to chase them away.

And remembering that terrible snarling buzz brought him back to the present, to the sound of other flies angrily circling another man, this time one who'd crossed the threshold far enough that he couldn't make it back.

Looking down at the dead man, his legs now splayed almost casually, as if someone had simply thrown away a scarecrow no longer needed, Cranshaw noticed for the first time what the man had looked like. Sandy-colored hair, a long mustache, distorted now by the bloated face, a scar, possibly from a saber, along his right cheek, starting at the right ear and ending almost on the point of the chin. Probably a nice enough looking man when he had been alive, which couldn't have been more recently than a week ago, and maybe even longer.

Cranshaw wanted to know who the man had been, but he couldn't bring himself to search the clothing for any stray bits of paper that might tell him. He could find out in town, if the people of Carney would talk to him. They didn't much like Rangers in this part of Texas. Lex knew that, and he was prepared for it. But one thing he wouldn't do was pretend. He wouldn't hide what he was, not even if it would make his job easier, because that was just too damn close to lying.

No sir, he wouldn't do that. He'd ride into Carney with the gun right there on his right hip. And he wasn't going to leave until he got what he came for. The nameless cadaver just five feet away was not the first, but if Lex Cranshaw had anything to say about it, it would be the last.

There had been three hangings in all. Three that he knew about, that is. And the wonder of it was that it had taken two more after the first before word filtered back to Austin. And prying the truth out from behind the clenched teeth in Carney was not going to be easy.

Now that he'd cut the man down, he wondered what to do. He didn't have a shovel, and there weren't enough rocks to do the job. Cranshaw moved back to his horse and was about to swing into the saddle when he heard an odd creaking sound. He let go of the reins and turned toward the noise. He didn't see anything at first. He backed away from the horse and stared down along the line of trees. He still didn't see anything, but the noise kept on coming.

A moment later, a team of mules, two, and then four, materialized a quarter-mile down the windbreak. There must be a gap in the trees, he thought. He could see the wagon now, an old schooner, its canvas stained and patched so often Cranshaw couldn't tell which was the original and which the patches.

The wagon made an awkward turn and headed in his direction. Cranshaw could see the driver, and as far as he could tell, the driver was alone. As the wagon pulled closer, he got a good look at the man on the reins. He appeared to be sixty-some, maybe even a little older. He had a thick shock of white hair and a beard to match. Cranshaw instinctively thought back to his mother's Bible, and the pictures of Moses and Abraham.

He stepped away from the trees and hailed the wagon.

The old man nodded to him as the wagon drew closer. When he was abreast of Cranshaw, the driver clucked to his animals, pulled the brake lever, and let his hands sit in his lap, the reins clutched loosely in a tangle of parchment-covered fingers.

Cranshaw stepped to the driver's side of the wagon and found himself pinned by the bluest, clearest eyes he'd ever seen. The leather skin above the beard made the eyes even more striking. They were young eyes in an ancient face. He was about to introduce himself when the old man spoke.

"See you met William," he said.

Cranshaw was confused for a moment. "William?" he asked.

The old man nodded toward the corpse. "Yonder," he said. "That's him. William."

"You know him?"

"Did."

"What's his name? His full name, I mean?"

"William Otterkill. William James Otterkill. People just called him William, though, or Billy. Like he didn't have no other name at all. Should have left him hangin', though, son."

"Why's that?"

"That's just the way it's supposed to be around here. Man get's himself strung up, he's supposed to hang around awhile. Who are you, anyway?"

Lex extended a hand. "Cranshaw. Lex Cranshaw."

The old man ignored the hand. "Well, Mr. Cranshaw, looks like you bit yourself a mouthful of trouble. You better chew it fast and get on away from here."

"I'm here because of the hangings. I . . . "

"I know what you are. Don't think I'm dumb just cause I'm old. But you got no business here. Ranger or not."

"What's your name? Who are you?"

"Jeremiah."

"Jeremiah what?"

"That'll do. You won't have no need of my last name. You won't be around long enough to use it."

"We'll see about that. You got a shovel in that wagon?"

"What for?"

"Got to bury this man. Can't leave him here like that."

Jeremiah nodded slowly. He looped the reins around the brake lever, then climbed down from the wagon seat. He moved easily, even gracefully. He strode back along the wagon bed and disappeared. Cranshaw heard the rattle of metal on metal. Jeremiah reappeared with a spade that looked to be as old as he was, and flipped it to Cranshaw.

"Better dig two holes, while you're at it, Mr. Cranshaw."

L EX watched the wagon creak away, its bed rocking from side to side. Long after it was out of sight around a bend in the tree line, he could still hear its wheels crying out for grease. The old man had told him nothing more, refusing to answer questions and volunteering nothing of his own, not even a comment on the weather, which was hotter than usual and drier than it ought to be.

Climbing up into the saddle, Lex looked at the mound of earth, darker than the rest of the soil. That was no way for a man to go, he thought, to be left like a piece of suet on a string, food for birds. And now, lying in an unmarked grave, William James Otterkill was on the verge of disappearing into oblivion. In two weeks, there would be nothing left but bones under the settled earth. A week later, weeds would have sprouted and a passerby wouldn't even notice the slight disturbance of the ground.

Hell, he thought, even common criminals get a headstone.

Carney was only four miles away, and it took Cranshaw about about an hour to reach the outskirts. Reining in next to a sign that advertised the town limits, he surveyed the dreary place with a jaundiced eye. He'd seen other collections of ramshackle buildings, enough like this one that he decided he already knew as much as he needed to about Carney.

There were two streets. They crossed in a rough "X," the buildings strung along both sides of its four arms. This was cattle country. It was hot and it was dry and, worst of all, it was dusty. As he nudged his roan forward again, he heard the little plops of its hooves in the thick layer of fine silt. Looking down, he watched the small puffs of dust exploding from under the hooves, drifting a few inches then settling back to earth.

Just looking at the place gave him a bad feeling. Carney, and towns like it, seemed to bring out the worst in men. Life was so close to the edge that only men and women who liked the thought of tipping over that edge completely managed to survive.

Lex measured towns by the number of saloons within their boundaries. The more saloons, the more liquor. The more liquor, the more violence. Carney was a five-saloon town. He was thirsty, and the inside of his mouth still tasted of the stench of William James Otterkill. He couldn't get the smell out of his nose.

He found the sheriff's office, and tied up in front. When

he entered, a big ruddy-faced man with black hair and blacker eyes watched him without saying anything. The man had hands like bear claws, and they sat on either side of the tattered blotter on the desk, the fingers curled in toward the palms.

"You Sheriff Harkness?" Lex asked. He saw the man's eyes linger for a moment on his gun.

"Who wants to know?"

Lex stuck out a hand. "Lex Cranshaw." The man behind the desk looked at the hand but made no move to grasp it.

"I'm Roy Harkness. What can I do for you?"

"I thought you already knew. I thought you'd be expecting me."

"Wasn't expecting nobody. Don't need nobody, so I had no reason to be expecting somebody, now did I?"

"But I was told that . . . "

"I don't give a damn what you were told. It's like I told them back in Austin. Leave us the hell alone. We can take care of our own trouble."

Lex nodded. "I saw that on the way in."

Harkness knit his brow for a second. "What do you mean?"

"I saw Otterkill. You know about that, don't you?"

"Course I do. Ever'body in these parts knows about Billy. Just about ever'body thinks it was a good thing, too. That's why they left him hangin'."

Cranshaw glanced around the office for a moment. Spotting a ladderback chair in one corner, he grabbed it by the back, twirled it around and sat down, his arms folded across the top of the chair. "I cut him down," Lex said.

"What for? You had no call to do that."

"It was indecent, sheriff. Civilized people don't do things like that."

"You sayin' we ain't civilized, Cranshaw?"

Lex shrugged. "I guess I'll find that out soon enough, won't I?"

"You won't be around here that long," Harkness said. He smiled. "Soon's you figure out we know what we're doing, you can go on back to Austin, or wherever the hell you come from."

"We'll see about that. You know what happened to Otterkill?"

"I know they stretched his mangy neck for 'im. I know that he probably had it coming or they wouldn't have. I know that much."

"You know who?"

Harkness shook his head. "Don't have any idea at all."

"You know why?"

"Hell, sure I do. He had it comin' that's why. Ever'body knows that. Otterkill was scum. He was rustling cattle from everbody with an acre or more."

"What about the others?"

"Now, what others would that be?"

"Claude Simmons and Wolf Berger . . . " Those were the names, according to Jeremiah, who hadn't told him much else. It seemed that communication was in short supply in Carney, like water and manners.

Harkness seemed off-balance for a moment. But he

recovered quickly. "I reckon Otterkill done that."

"But you don't know for sure?"

"Mr. Cranshaw, I am a busy man. I have had a belly full of your damn questions. I already told you, we can handle our own business. Now, if you'll excuse me, I have work to do." Harkness got up and pushed his chair back so hard it slammed into the wall behind him. He stepped around the desk and stood glowering down at Cranshaw. "You mind? I got to lock up."

Lex took a deep breath. When he stood up, Harkness still towered over him by half a foot. The sheriff was a good inch or two over six feet, and weighed better than two hundred pounds. He waited impatiently for Lex to leave.

Lex started toward the door. He was almost through the doorway when he stopped and turned. "Otterkill have any family around here?"

Harkness screwed his close-set eyes even closer together, as if he were certain it was a trick question but couldn't quite decide how. "Some," he said. "Sulfur Valley, somewheres, I think. Maybe you should go bother them for a while."

"Thank you. Maybe I will."

Harkness grunted something, then followed Lex through the doorway and onto the boardwalk. He pulled the door closed with a bang that rattled the glass in its frame. Trying the knob to make sure it had locked, he turned to Cranshaw. "You learn anything, anything at all, you let me hear about it, you understand?"

Lex nodded. "I'll do that, sheriff, I surely will."

"See that you do."

It was apparent Harkness wanted the last word, so Lex didn't bother to respond. He stepped into the dusty street and walked around the hitching post. Untying his reins, he stood with one foot in the stirrup, watching the sheriff lumber along the boardwalk toward the north end of town.

He veered left, and Cranshaw watched the butterfly doors of a saloon flutter to a standstill before climbing into the saddle. He had the feeling he was going to be around Carney a little longer than he'd expected, and a lot longer than Roy Harkness would like.

There was a small hotel in town, but it was over a saloon, and he preferred a little more quiet. The clerk directed him to a boarding house, a mile or so out the south end of town. He tied up in front and walked onto the porch. Unlike most of the buildings in the town, this one showed signs of maintenance. There was a recent coat of paint on the walls, and a pair of barrels, each cut into two, had been converted to flower pots. The four were strung out across the front of the place, dripping ivy over their sides. Some red flowers, geraniums he thought, looked well tended. The clincher was the porch. It was free of dust, as if it had been swept within the past day or so. That alone was enough to set it apart from the other buildings of Carney.

He knocked on the door and a voice called "hello" from somewhere. He was about to knock again when a woman appeared at one end of the porch. She was carrying a broom, and her hair was covered with a kerchief.

"Hello," she said again. "Can I help you?"

"I was wondering if you had a room available," Lex said.

The woman nodded, then moved to the porch steps and climbed up. She was limping, he noticed, not badly, but enough that he spotted it immediately. Once on the porch, she extended a hand. When he took it, the grip was firm and muscular.

She dropped his hand suddenly. Taking off the kerchief, she shook out her hair, which was long and curly. In the sunlight, its light brown color looked almost like polished copper, Lex thought.

"You're here about Billy, aren't you?"

"Ma'am?"

"William Otterkill. He's why you're here, isn't he?"

"What makes you think that?"

She shrugged. He couldn't tell whether it was to hide something she knew or because it was only common sense and she expected any reasonable person to know it.

Cranshaw thought back to the poorly scrawled letter he'd seen, warning of what was happening in Carney. It had been unsigned, and Captain Carmody had almost tossed it away, but there had been something about it, about the urgency of the language, about the obvious sincerity, that had caused him to hesitate. He'd shown it to Lex and left it up to him. Thinking back to that barely legible scrawl, he knew there was no way in hell this dignified woman had written it.

"I see you're no more talkative than anyone else around here," he said.

"It's not a good idea to say too much about that sort of thing."

"Why not?"

"It's a long story, Mr. . . . ?"

"Cranshaw. Lex Cranshaw."

"Let me show you to your room." She pushed open the front door and walked inside. Cranshaw followed her. The place was as neat inside as it was tidy outside. It smelled of cut flowers. She led the way to the second floor and down a corridor to the last room on the left.

The door was open, and he stepped in after her, finding himself in a bright and airy chamber. Lace curtains on the windows were held back with ties, and there were cut flowers in a glass vase on an oak dresser.

"I hope it suits you, Mr. Cranshaw."

"How much is it?"

"For you, no charge."

"Ma'am, I can't . . . "

"Nonsense, Mr. Cranshaw. I insist. It's the least I can do."

"Do about what, Mrs. . . . ?"

"Helderson, Elizabeth Helderson. And it's Miss."

"Do about what, Miss Helderson?"

"You'll know. Soon enough, you'll know."

BILLY Otterkill had family, such as it was, on a small spread six miles from Carney. When Lex had inquired whether Otterkill had any surviving kin, noses wrinkled in distaste. More than one man had spat in the dust, none too casually, and not that far from the toes of Cranshaw's boots. That Billy was almost universally disliked was only half of it. That there had to be a reason was the other half, but nobody wanted to elaborate.

As he rode out of Carney the next morning, he was aware of people watching him. Conversations died as he rode past, faces turned to follow him and more than one pair of eyes tracked his departure from behind lace curtains.

On the road out in the arid land surrounding Carney, Lex could still feel the hostility. Whatever had turned the people of Carney against Billy Otterkill, they not only didn't give a damn that he was dead, they apparently didn't much want to see anything happen to those who killed him. And that made Lex Cranshaw just as unpopular as the man whose murder he came to avenge.

The sun was already well up in the sky, and the heat made everything shimmer in front of him. The few trees looked as if they had been dried and bleached. Even the leaves were a pale yellow, as if it hadn't rained in a year and the trees were barely hanging on. The air was full of angry flies buzzing in close to try and draw a little blood, and Lex was kept busy waving them away. The air looked as if it had turned yellow, too, and every step of the horse kicked up more yellow dust, so fine it swirled in the air in an unbroken stream, the way the color of tea swirled away from the leaves until the whole cup was dyed amber.

Two miles out, he saw some range cattle off to the left in a shallow depression full of brittle willows. The cattle were almost lifeless, just their tails flicking at flies, the cud chewed in slow motion.

On a hunch, Lex veered left, slowing his horse as he approached the cattle. From thirty yards, he could see they'd been branded, and as he drew closer, the cattle watched him warily, their eyes fixed on him, the swishing of the tails the only sound other than the clop of his mount's hooves on the dry ground.

Dismounting, he moved close to the edge of the small clump of skinny beeves. They were skittish, and he moved slowly, crooning to the frightened cows until he got close enough to see the brand. It was an odd design, a rocking

U, but the *u* was wider than it should be. Lex knelt beside the cow and ran his fingers over the scarred hide. One leg of the *u* was slightly wider than the other, but only halfway up.

Straightening, he checked the earmark. There was something odd about it, too. Two notches, side by side, had been cut into the cow's ear, but one looked fresher than the other, as if someone had cut it long after the first.

Lex moved among the steers, which now seemed to have accepted him, or at least decided he was no threat to them. All had the same odd earmark and the same brand. But the brand on some was perfect, on others, the right leg of the *u* had that odd hitch in it halfway up.

He wasn't sure why it meant something, or what it meant, but there was no doubt in his mind it was significant. Back in Carney he'd have to ask around, see who owned the "Rocking U." He was walking back to his mount when he heard something, a bee, maybe, zip past his ear, and he was reaching up to swat it away when the crack registered.

The bullet had narrowly missed him. Instinctively, he hit the deck, crabwalking back toward the cattle. They had heard the gunshot, and were looking around, beginning to fidget. Close to the cattle he had the extra cover of the overhanging willows, but he still had no idea where the shooter was hidden.

Another bullet slammed into the nearest willow trunk, scattering clipped leaves over his head and shoulders. This time he got a fix on the gunshot. Squinting in the bright sun, he looked for the shooter, or some cover he might hide behind. Nothing jumped out at him. Scattered boulders and stunted thornbush here and there offered some cover, but not much.

Lex backed toward the willow trunk and took a look at the bullet hole. It was fairly large, too large for an ordinary rifle. Probably a buffalo gun, he thought, a Sharps or a Remington.

He was surprised that someone should be after him so soon. It could mean only that he was too close to something, or that somebody was running scared. But if he was close to something, he had no idea what it might be.

Putting the willow between himself and the shooter, he sorted through his options. Waiting was the easiest, but it was also the riskiest. He had no idea how many men were out there in the arid flats, and he couldn't take the initiative until he knew. He could make a run for it, but that didn't sit well with him. He knew Colonel Hays wouldn't have run, and neither would Lee Hall.

It was quiet again. The seconds ticked off in his mind, then the minutes. The slap and swish of the ropey tails of the cattle was the only sound. Lex looked at his horse, trying to decide whether he could make it to the big roan without stopping a bullet. He knew it was a long shot, but he didn't seem to have any real choice.

Steeling himself for the sprint, he heard the distant slap of hooves and ducked into the open. The sunlight was so brilliant, he could barely keep his eyes focused. The hoofbeats were retreating, but he still couldn't see a thing.

Dashing for his mount, he vaulted into the saddle and dug in his spurs. The big roan leapt forward, and was in full gallop in seconds. Lex could no longer hear the gunman's horse, and he still couldn't see anything. Charging headlong in the general direction of the sound, he finally spotted a thin plume of dust, drifting like a pale feather across his line of sight.

Off to the left, he noticed a clump of mesquite, its dense, spiked branches twisted and knotted together into one impenetrable wall. He slowed his horse to a walk, and swept the ground with his eyes as he drifted toward the mesquite patch.

He saw the hoofprints almost immediately. A patch of ground had been kicked and scarred by impatient hooves. Dismounting, Lex knelt beside the edge of the trampled patch. He could see bootprints now, too. The edge of one sole was notched, and there was an oval mound dead center where the sole had been worn away.

Letting go of the reins, he crept forward, looking for something he could use. He almost missed it. Half buried in the dust, tight up under the mesquite, a spent cartridge casing, its empty nose a black hole in the yellow dust, caught his eye. Carefully avoiding the thorns, Lex slid his hand in far enough to grab the empty shell and pull it out.

It was a Sharps. The powerful 90-load and 500-grain slug were designed to stop a buffalo bull under a full head of steam. It would have torn his head off if the shooter had been a better marksman. Lex tucked the spent shell into his pocket, and walked slowly back to his horse. Swinging up into the saddle, he decided his visit to Billy Otterkill's kin could wait. The gunman had left a trail, and it would never be any hotter than it was now.

Urging his horse into a trot, he watched the ground, following the blurry hoofprints with a practiced eye. He knew he might be heading right back under the muzzle of the Sharps, but it didn't seem likely. The gunman had fled without a challenge from Lex, so it wouldn't make sense for him to set up somewhere down the trail. Whoever it was had run to get away, not to lead him on.

As he expected, the trail led Lex right back to Carney. The shooter had taken the most direct route, not bothering with what passed for a road. That made Cranshaw's job a little easier. The gunman's horse was the only one to pass that way. On the road, the tracks might have blended in with others, maybe been obliterated altogether. That seemed odd, almost as if the shooter didn't care whether he had been followed or not.

Lex started to wonder whether he might have been wrong, whether the gunman had set another ambush, or maybe was leading him under the guns of accomplices. But there was only one way to find out for sure.

By ten thirty, the town was already in sight. As he drew closer, everything seemed normal. There was some traffic in the streets, and as he reined in to think through his next move, a buckboard creaked up behind him. Lex turned in the saddle, but the driver ignored his wave.

Lex watched the old man snap the reins, pushing his team harder than necessary. The driver never turned, didn't even flick his eyes toward Lex as he drove past.

The man's face was leathery and dark from the sun, but it was smooth, like the skin of a much younger man. Black eyes glittered like two pieces of polished coal under the shaggy gray eyebrows. The lips were set in a thin line, like those of a carpenter holding the last nail as he climbed a ladder.

When the wagon was past him, Lex goaded his mount in behind it. The tracks of the gunman were lost in the gouged earth of the busy street, and there was no point in pretending he could follow them any farther. But he had something to go on, now.

Lex tied off in front of a saloon, the Flying Dutchman, and leaned on the rail for a moment. A half-dozen horses were already hitched to one of the two rails, but he didn't want to seem interested in anything just yet. He was waiting for the curious eyes to lose interest. He rolled a cigarette, lit it with a wooden match, then puffed contentedly. When the cigarette was finished, he ground the butt under his heel and climbed onto the boardwalk in front of the saloon.

None of the horses at the rail seemed to have been ridden hard. One by one, he checked the boot on each mount, but there was no Sharps. Lex stepped back into the street and drifted along, checking one mount after another. Two were still overheated, but neither had a buffalo gun in the boot. Either the bushwhacker had ridden straight on through town, or he'd put his horse out of sight.

Working his way back down the opposite side of the main street, he moved down an alley between a hardware store and one of the town's five saloons. Out behind the buildings he found the usual litter, bleached timbers, broken crates, a mound of something or other covered with faded canvas. But no horse.

Lex moved back to the main street and headed for Mitchell's General Store. People passed him, and, it seemed to Lex, gave him a little more room than he needed, as if they were afraid they might catch something from him.

The store was empty when he stepped in out of the sun. It felt cool, and after the brilliant sunlight it seemed darker than it was. He heard some rattling behind the counter, and he called out, "Anyone here?"

The rattling stopped and a moment later a head appeared in a doorway behind the counter.

"What can I do you for?" the head asked. Then the body to which it was attached slowly filled the doorway. The man was almost as big across as he was up and down, his bulk wrapped in a dark blue apron with pockets bulging all across its front.

Lex walked to the counter. "Morning," he said.

"Looking for something particular?" the man asked.

"Could be."

The storekeeper waited, then stuck out a hand the size of a small roast beef. Lex grabbed the pudgy fingers and the storekeeper smiled. "Don't think we've met," he said. "You're that Ranger, ain't you? Name's Mitchell, Martin S., but I don't use the S. Fact is, I don't use the Martin, either. Folks call me Mitch."

"Lex Cranshaw."

"You're here about them hangin's, ain't you?"

Lex nodded.

"Terrible thing," Mitchell said. "Course, it's no big surprise."

"Why's that?"

Mitchell waved a hand. "You know how it is. Nothing particular. Not really, anyhow. Just a feeling. Like something had to happen."

Lex backed off, storing the information away until he had a little more to go on. "Looking for a buffalo gun. A Sharps, if possible."

Mitchell shook his head. "Haven't had one in stock for a long time. No call for it."

"Know anybody might have one he'd want to sell?"

"I could ask around for you, you want. It'll be steep though, maybe a hundred dollars or thereabouts."

Lex noticed the stock of ammunition on a shelf behind the counter. There were two boxes of .44–90–500 shells. He didn't call attention to them. "No need," he said. "Thanks for your time."

IT was late afternoon when Lex reined in on the crest of a low hill. In the shallow valley below, he could see the Otterkill place, spread out like a green stain on a beige tablecloth. Whatever else the Otterkills did, they had a way with plants. The house had seen better days, or maybe not. Maybe it had been built out of the ruins of houses that had. The walls were bare lumber, shades of charcoal gray streaking the paler gray here and there.

A ramshackle barn, its own boards no friendlier with paint than the house itself, seemed to lean on an angle so precarious that the first gust of wind might send it tumbling over on its side. There was a fence, split rails every bit as forlorn as the buildings, and some of the rails were halfway down, their lower halves lost in a tangle of weeds.

There was a small corral alongside the barn, and unlike the rest of the place, it looked as if it were well-tended.

Lex eased down the hillside toward the yawning gate. As he passed through it, the scent of flowers swirled around him. Beyond the fence on either side, bean poles, already smothered in the climbing vines, stalks of corn, and a dozen other vegetables, marched in neat rows parallel to the fence. At the far edge, stands of hollyhock, the thick-petaled red and purple flowers half hidden under clouds of bees, leaned against the fence, itself drowning in honeysuckle and wisteria.

Lex couldn't reconcile the apparent concern lavished on the garden with the neglect of the house and out-buildings. But he pushed the puzzle aside. It was just one more thing about human nature he'd have to think about, someday when he had the time.

He dismounted in front of the rickety-looking porch and tied up at a hitching post almost too fragile to bear the weight of the reins. He called hello, but got no answer. As he walked toward the porch, his spurs clinking dully in the hot afternoon air, he watched the window to the left of the peeling planks of the front door.

He put one boot on the porch and leaned forward, letting his bent knee take his weight. Reaching out with his left hand, he rapped on one of the hollow pillars trying to support the porch roof. The dull thump, like that of an empty keg, echoed off the front of the house.

He called again, and again got no answer.

Climbing the two stairs to the porch, he knocked on the front door. The planks rattled under his fist. Still no one answered him.

Lex stepped back off the porch and walked around

back, but the house looked just as deserted, and no better maintained, from the rear. Lex stepped close to the curtainless window set dead center, and leaned close, shielding his eyes from the reflected glare with a curved palm. The glass was dusty, and half a dozen bubbles in the thick, greenish pane distorted everything inside. He wiped some of the dust away, then looked again. There was no movement inside, and no sign that anyone had been there recently.

Moving past the end of the house, he walked toward the barn. Its front doors were wide open, but the interior was dark. He leaned through to call hello, but only his own voice answered him, echoing from high in the rafters. He took a step or two inside. The dank, musty smell of decaying hay assailed his nostrils and he suppressed the urge to gag.

A horse nickered somewhere outside, and Lex backed through the barn door, thinking maybe someone had come home. But the yard was as empty as it had been. The horses in Otterkill's corral seemed nervous about something, and Lex loosened the Colt on his hip, just in case.

He started back to the house when he heard the telltale click of a Winchester lever. "You lookin' for somebody?"

Lex turned slowly, knowing the sights would be leveled somewhere on the middle of his back and the finger on the trigger might be a touch skittish.

He found himself staring down the barrel of a rifle at a young man who couldn't have been twenty, and might not even be seventeen. Brown hair, soft as a baby's, dropped over his forehead. His blue eyes were wide, and his mouth was still soft, like the chubby cheeks.

"Looking for Mr. Otterkill," he said.

"Which one?"

"Any one will do. You kin?"

"Son and brother," the kid said. "What you want?"

Smiling to put the kid at ease, Lex said, "My name's Cranshaw. Lex Cranshaw." As he spoke he started to step toward the kid, who waved the muzzle slightly.

"Don't need to come no closer, Cranshaw," the kid said. He was trying to make his voice sound hard, but it cracked once, and the kid coughed to try and hide it.

Lex noticed the kid's knuckles were white, and he raised both hands in the air, palms forward. "Don't need that rifle, son."

"That ain't for you to decide." It was a new voice, deeper, and harder-edged. Lex turned to look over his shoulder in time to see a larger, leaner version of the kid step out from behind a corner of the house.

"Look," Cranshaw said, "I . . . "

"No, you look. You're trespassin'. Be best you git on out of here. Paw, you tell him . . . "

A third man appeared as if from nowhere. He was much older than the first two, but looking at the craggy face, Lex knew what the others would look like if they lived long enough to be as old. It was almost spooky, seeing the three faces so different, and yet so much alike.

And it dawned on him only slowly. Thinking back to his first day in Carney, that moment when William James Otterkill had spun half around on the end of his rope. It was the same face, no doubt about it. In his mind, Lex withdrew the death-blackened tongue, filled the gory sockets with a pair of soft blue eyes, and it was just one more pea in the same pod.

The old man crossed the yard, taking care not to get between Lex and the muzzle of either rifle. He tilted his head to one side a bit, like a confused hawk will do. "You got no business here, Mr. Cranshaw. None at all."

"That's not how I see it, Mr. Otterkill."

"Don't matter how you see it. Not to me it don't. And not to mine, neither. Me and the boys can take care of ourselves. We don't need no help."

"But . . . ."

"No, Mr. Cranshaw. Don't need no help. No Otterkill ever does. And Issac sure don't."

"I take it you're Isaac?"

"Take whatever you want, so long's you take it some-wheres else."

"I just want to ask you a few questions."

"No need."

"But there is, Mr. Otterkill. Somebody's got to put an end to the hangings around here. Three is three too many."

"Maybe so, maybe so. But it won't stop at three, Cran-shaw. Might not stop at four, neither. All depends on how many strung my Billy up. The hangins'll end all right, but not until ever' last one of them bastards gets to dangle awhile."

"I'm afraid I can't allow that, Mr. Otterkill."

"You got nothin' to say about it. I know who you are,

and I know why you're here. But you don't belong here, you got no business here and you got no right. I mean to take care of them what hung my Billy, and if I got to shoot you to keep you from interfering, well, that's just how it'll be."

"Then you know who's responsible?"

"Sure I know. I knowed as soon as I heard what happened. I warned Billy to be careful, so I guess maybe it's my fault for not seein' to it he did. But it's too late to worry about that end of it now. Now I got to make 'em pay. And as sure as there's supposed to be a God in heaven, I will do that, Mr. Texas Ranger Cranshaw or not. You understand?"

Lex nodded. "I understand. But you better understand something, too, Mr. Otterkill. The law has something to say about it. If you think you can go around it, or ignore it, or just plain trample on it, you better think again. If you know who killed your boy and you don't tell me, I will still find out. One way or another, I will find out. And if anything happens to that man, I will hold you responsible, and you will do some hanging of your own, all nice and legal-like. You can bank on that."

"You just shut up," the leaner boy snarled. "Shut up or I'll shut you up."

"Lucas, you mind your manners." The old man swiped at his son with the back of one weathered hand. "Cranshaw's just doin' what he's supposed to do. You've no call to talk to him like that."

"But Paw, I . . ."

This time the hand connected. Lucas went sprawling in

the dust. He lay there a moment, stunned, then wiped at his mouth with the back of one hand. The bloody drool smeared across his chin and the back of his hand. He looked at it, then at Lex. He spat in the dirt, then got to his knees.

Otterkill looked at Lex. "You got to keep boys in line or they'll run wild on you. I learned that from their Maw. And I always done it, even after Lettie passed. That's how come I know Billy never done nothing to deserve what happened to him. And because I know that, I mean to make it right."

"Another hanging won't make anything right, Mr. Otterkill."

"It'll make it so I can sleep nights."

"Why'd you let him hang there like that? Your own damn son. Why in hell didn't you give him a decent burial?"

"Buryin' him wouldn'ta changed nothing. The boy's dead. It was you cut him down, and I appreciate that. But it still don't change nothing. I got to do what I got to do."

"So do I, Mr. Otterkill. So do I."

"I understand. You best get on your horse and ride out of here now, Mr. Cranshaw. But I expect I'll see you again."

"You can count on it."

Otterkill turned to his older son. "Daniel, you git on in the house now, and be quick about it."

"I still say we ought to shoot him now, while we got the chance."

"Daniel, I ain't gone tell you again. We got no quarrel with Mr. Cranshaw. Git on in the house, now."

Daniel shrugged his shoulders. He never took his eyes off Lex as he backed toward the porch then climbed onto it, still walking backwards until he bumped into the front door.

When the door closed with a loud bang, Isaac looked at Lucas, who scrambled to his feet again and brought his rifle back to bear on the middle of Cranshaw's body. Lex watched the kid, who peered at him along the barrel of his rifle. The kid never blinked, but his Adam's apple bobbed with every swallow. The kid was scared stiff, and doing his best to hide it.

"Lucas," Issac said. "You show Mr. Cranshaw back to town, you hear me?"

"Yes, Paw."

"And you be courteous."

"I will, Paw."

Isaac nodded. To Lex, he said, "He's a good boy. Just like Billy was. He won't give you no trouble, as long as you don't give him none."

Isaac backed away a couple of steps, sweeping his hand toward Cranshaw's horse. Lex nodded and walked to his mount. With one foot in the stirrups, he paused for a moment. He turned to Isaac, who was still watching him closely. "You tell Sheriff Harkness who hung Billy?"

Isaac snorted. "You don't look like the sort of man who'd set a fox to watch his henhouse, Mr. Cranshaw. Neither am I."

LEX Cranshaw had a lot to think about. It was beginning to look like just about everyone in Carney knew who had been responsible for Billy Otterkill's death. Everyone except Lex Cranshaw, that is. And it was just as certain that no one was prepared to tell him. He'd been through this sort of thing before. It would slow him down, but it sure as hell wouldn't stop him. There were a few tricks in his bag yet, and if the bag got empty, he'd find another bag.

As Carney came into view he felt his gut tighten. He hadn't realized until that moment just how angry he was. The people were so damned stubborn, but there was one person in town who wanted the lunacy to end. Somebody, after all, had written to Austin. The letter hadn't been signed, but it had made enough of an impression on the brass hats that Lex had been dispatched to look into the matter.

Not that lynchings were that unusual. Hell, a place as big as Texas, with as few lawmen and as much rope, was bound to have an occasional man swinging from a tree limb. It didn't make it right, but it did seem logical, somehow. Texas was hard country. It was full of hard men and the rules were well known, whether anybody had bothered to write them down or not.

But how did the rules apply to Billy Otterkill? What, if anything, had he done, and to whom had he done it? And, perhaps most important of all, who in hell was it who was worried enough to write to the capital? Harkness said Billy was rustling cattle. But he hadn't said how he knew it. For that matter, he hadn't said whose cattle they were.

Lex needed to unwind, and as the first dilapidated buildings slid by on his right, he decided there was only one place to do it and do it right. He let the horse find its own way to the center of town, then jerked the reins and walked his mount to the hitching post in front of the Flying Dutchman.

Judging by the horses crammed together in front of the place, it was going to be crowded. It was a Friday night, and the end of the month, which meant there would be more than a few slack jaws inside, their hinges well-greased by the shag-end of a month's pay.

But that might not be so bad, Lex thought as he dismounted. A cowboy with a little juice in his belly just might talk a little more than he ought to. One thing might lead to another. Lex snugged the reins on the end of the post and walked up to the butterfly doors. He stood on tiptoe and looked inside, one hand on either door. The place was jammed already. He shoved open the doors and stepped inside. Until that moment, he hadn't realized just how noisy the place was. He knew it then, because the noise came to an abrupt end.

Lex almost grinned. It was a reaction he'd gotten used to, and he remembered once talking to Will Jason, before he'd been killed in San Antonio, about how the neck bones creaked so loud when all the heads in a bar swiveled at one time. Will had said the sound was like one big rusty hinge groaning. There'd be a hundred eyes staring at you and fifty pairs of stiff, white lips. Then somebody'd say something, louder than he had to, and things would slowly get loud again, but it was never the same after that. You were always aware that somebody was watching you, trying to figure whether you were there for him or not, and the eyes would get glassy as their owner tried to figure what to do.

Times like this, Lex found himself thinking of Will. It had been just such a bar where someone had slipped up alongside Will and slit him from belt to brisket with a Bowie knife. He had been just thirty-three years old, not much older than Lex was now. And the bastard who'd done it cheated the gallows by hanging himself in his cell. That had been six years ago, and there wasn't a single day Lex hadn't thought about the man who taught him the tricks of the trade, and kept him alive long enough to master them.

Looking around the room, Lex found an empty table in one corner. There still wasn't a sound as he crossed the floor, his spurs jingling with every step. When he reached the table, he pulled a chair around and slipped in behind the whiskey-stained tablecloth, lowered himself to the chair and put up a hand for a waiter.

Then, predictable as the chimes on a Swiss clock, somebody cracked a bad joke, somebody else laughed, and pretty soon the conversation was back to its freight-train roar. But they were still watching him out of the corners of their eyes, spitting the words out of lips twisted to one side.

A fragile little man in striped shirt and sleeve garters drifted toward him, his head twisting back over his shoulder, then toward Lex and back over his shoulder again. The closer he got to Cranshaw's table, the slower he moved. Lex waited patiently, his hands folded on the soiled tabletop, his thumbs circling one another like mating birds.

Finally, when he could avoid it no longer, the little man planted himself across the table from Lex. He was leaning back so far Lex feared the waiter might fall on his butt.

"Ye-ye-yessir. Wh-what c-c-can I g-get you?" Lex smiled at the stutter, and the little man got mad. For a moment, he forget about the people watching him, and he repeated his question, this time with a confidence born of irritation. "What can I get you?"

"Bourbon. Kentucky bourbon. Bring the whole damn bottle."

Lex watched the room instead of the waiter. Each pair

of eyes he saw danced away from his gaze, flicked back to make sure his scrutiny had passed on and, if it hadn't, danced away again.

"Ye-yessir." The stutter was back, but Lex didn't smile this time. He stared hard at the waiter until he turned his back and moved reluctantly toward the bar.

Lex watched as the waiter struggled through the crowd until he could get close enough to relay the order to the bartender. One of the men in the crowd, nearly a head taller than the waiter, and a good couple of inches taller than anybody in the room, laid a heavy hand on the waiter's shoulder, then leaned down to whisper something.

The waiter shook his head once, then again more vigorously.

The bartender slapped an unopened bottle of bourbon on the bar, slid it to the front edge and waited until the waiter closed his hand over the neck. As he backed away, the waiter tripped. Lex saw the big man's foot draw back and one big hand close over the bottle as the waiter fell to the floor.

A woman in a bright blue dress, a fan of small, brightly colored feathers arranged in her hair, snatched the bottle from the cowboy's grip and said something Lex didn't catch. The cowhand scowled, but the men in his immediate vicinity all laughed as the woman turned smartly and pranced across the floor toward Lex.

"You mind a little company?" she said, setting the bottle on the table.

Lex shook his head. "Suit yourself."

"I usually do." She sat down across from him and slit the paper seal on the bourbon with one long, brightly painted thumbnail. "I'm Delilah," she said. She smiled what appeared to be a genuine smile.

When Lex didn't respond, she continued, "And you're Lex Cranshaw."

He still didn't answer. She smiled again, more cautiously this time. "I don't usually have to use forceps to get a kind word from a man," she said.

"You invited yourself," he said.

"So I did." She grinned. "You're not the most popular man in this little hellhole of a town, you know."

Lex grunted. When the paper was slit all the way around, Delilah twisted the cork free and reached into her dress and pulled out a pair of small crystal glasses. Setting them down on the table, she poured three fingers of bourbon in each. Looking at him as she poured the second, she asked, "You don't mind, do you?"

"Does it make any difference?"

She laughed then. It was a rich and husky sound coming from someplace deep inside her. "No, it doesn't."

Setting the bottle down, she pushed a glass across the rumpled cotton of the tablecloth, then lifted the second in her delicate fingers. She held it to her lips for a moment, then gestured toward him. He watched the dark amber fluid slip up the side of the glass almost to the rim, and reached for his own glass.

"Salute," she said, taking a sip. Lex nodded.

He was watching the crowd at the bar. The big cowboy was staring at him. Carrying on a conversation out of the side of his mouth, he kept his eyes on Lex every second. So, when he finally detached himself from the other hands, Lex wasn't surprised.

The big man stood behind Delilah, put one heavy hand on her shoulder and pulled her and her chair back away from the table. Lex tensed, but he tried not to let it show.

"Hey," Delilah said, "what's the big idea?"

"Maybe you better run along upstairs, Lilah. It ain't fit for a lawman to be seen with a woman of your reputation, don't you know that?"

Lex stuck his tongue in his left cheek. "Maybe she wants to stay," he said. "Maybe her reputation is safer with me than it is with you."

"I wasn't talkin' to you," the cowhand said. He rubbed his scraggly mustache with one gloved finger. His brown eyes never wavered. His sunken cheeks, their skin turned to copper by the Texas sun, quivered slightly, as if he were angry about something but unwilling to have anyone know it.

"We weren't talking to you, either," Lex pointed out.

"Mason, you shouldn't . . . "

He slapped her then. The sound echoed from the high-beamed ceiling in the sudden silence. "I said hush up, Lilah," he snapped.

Lex stood up. "I think maybe you ought to run along, old son, before you do something you'll regret."

"You got no call to be tellin' me what to do."

"The hell I haven't."

The woman tried to step past the cowhand. She grabbed him by the arm, trying to turn him. "Mason, I . . ."

"I told you, Lilah, git!"

She looked at Lex, her lower lip trembling, as if she saw something bad was about to happen, something she felt responsible for. Mason jerked his arm free, then brought it back in a sharp arc. The blow caught the woman in the midsection and she doubled over.

Lex cleared the table and drove his shoulder hard into Mason's chest, driving him backward halfway to the bar, before both men collapsed in a heap. Mason cursed as he tried to scramble free, but Lex grabbed a fistful of shirt and twisted it into a knotted ball just under Mason's chin. With his right hand, he drew his Colt and slashed it down sharply, catching Mason on the temple. The sharp crack of metal on bone sounded like a pistol shot. Mason's head sagged to one side, and Lex let go of the man's shirt.

Straightening, he swept the bar with his gaze, engaging one pair of eyes after another, then passing on until every man in the place had turned away. Lex felt the knotted muscle writhing along his jawbone. He holstered the Colt and stepped back to help Delilah to her feet.

"You all right?" he asked.

She nodded. "I think so. But you better leave. Mason's an ugly drunk."

"He's sleeping it off right now. When he wakes up, I figure he'll leave me be."

"I'd watch my back, if I was you. From now on."

"You got something you want to tell me, don't you?" His blue eyes bored into her, and she shrank away from his gaze.

She shook her head, a quick, almost invisible gesture.

Then she shook it harder. "No, nothing." She backed away then, turned and ran for the stairs. A moment later, she was out of sight.

Lex tossed a few bills on the bar, hooked the bourbon bottle with one hand and tossed off the rest of his drink in a single swallow. He could still taste the sourness of Carney against the back of his teeth. It would take more than bourbon to wash it away. But it was a start.

ELIZABETH Helderson set the blackened coffeepot on a thick slab of oak in the center of the table. Lex watched her, admiring the grace of her movement. The two other boarders watched her with something a little more aggressive. She seemed not to notice. As she walked back to the kitchen, one of the boarders, a thick-waisted man in a gray suit and muttonchop whiskers winked at Lex.

"Fine-looking woman, that Liz is."

Lex nodded.

"Like to give her a tumble, I would. How about you?"

Lex frowned, but the man didn't pay any attention. Instead, he nudged the other boarder, a tiny man with spidery fingers dancing nervously around the edge of his plate. "How about you, Carson? You like our hostess pretty well, don't you?" The man in the gray suit laughed a phlegmy laugh, cleared his throat, then stuck one thick finger under his collar to loosen it. His face was red and his neck showed the scrape of a dull razor. He turned back to Lex and said, "What line of work are you in?"

Lex didn't answer, but it didn't faze the man in the gray suit, who stuck a paw across the table, nearly knocking over a vase of cut flowers. "Pat Tunney," he said. "Dry goods is my line."

Lex took the hand without enthusiasm. When he let it go, Tunney tilted his head toward the smaller man. "This here is Winslow Carson. He's a music teacher, if you can believe that."

Carson stuck out a delicate hand that looked like it had been stripped of all flesh and the feathery white skin shrunken to fit the bones tightly. Lex shook hands again, again without enthusiasm. He was about to say something to be polite when Elizabeth Helderson reappeared. She set a platter of ham and fried eggs on another slab of oak, then took a seat at the head of the table.

"Mighty fine spread you put on this morning, Liz." Tunney grinned like a hungry wolf, reaching for the platter at the same time. This time he knocked the vase harder and Lex snatched it just before it fell. A few drops of water splattered the tablecloth and one hit the coffee-pot and sputtered into steam.

"Sorry about that, Liz," Tunney said.

"I believe it's Elizabeth," Carson said.

Tunney slapped him on the back. "Nonsense, we're all friends here. Right, Liz?" He winked at her, but she made no sign she'd seen it.

Lex said, "Miss Helderson is probably used to that kind of rudeness, but I don't think she likes it. I know I don't."

Tunney glared at him. "Aren't you the fine gentleman, then, eh?"

Lex stared at the fat man until he'd made his point, then reached for the coffee. He poured a cup for Miss Helderson, one for himself, then filled the others.

Tunney started on the ham and eggs, taking a rather generous amount before letting go of the platter and passing it to Carson. The music teacher pointedly offered it to Miss Helderson, who shook her head. "You go ahead, Mr. Carson. I can wait my turn."

When the platter reached Lex, he took two thick slices of the meat and was sliding a pair of eggs onto his plate when someone rapped sharply on the front door.

"Elizabeth, you there? Elizabeth?" The rapping grew louder and more impatient as she got to her feet and started toward the door. "Elizabeth?" Again frenetic rapping followed the call.

She turned the thumb-latch and pulled the door open as a bony fist once more descended on the thick glass. A creature half woman and half bird, all frail bones and fluttering limbs, flitted into the room. "Have you heard, Elizabeth? Did you hear? It's just awful."

"Dorothy, it's barely seven. I haven't been out of the house. How could I have heard anything? What in heaven's name are you talking about?" She looked apologetically at her boarders, then turned back to her visitor.

"The hangin's, Elizabeth, two of 'em. Last night."

Lex dropped his fork. No one seemed to notice the

clatter as he got to his feet. "Two men hanged, you say? Where?"

Delighted at having an avid listener, Dorothy fluttered toward Lex, her huge eyes bulging out of the pale, drawn face. "South of town, along the Beaver Fork. In the trees there. Two of 'em."

"Who were they?"

Dorothy shook her head, her face suddenly a mask of profound disappointment. "I don't know. I don't know if anybody knows, not yet, anyhow. The sheriff is goin' now to see about 'em."

Lex looked at Elizabeth Helderson. "You'll excuse me, Ma'am." He balled his napkin, wiped his lips on it, then tossed it on the table.

"Where in hell are you goin'?" Tunney bellowed.

But Lex was already out the door. He saddled his horse in a hurry, the big roan looking back at him as if wondering what all the fuss was about. He hit the saddle and dug in his spurs. Already, he could see the dust cloud that had to be Harkness on his way to the scene.

Lex caught up, and fell in beside the sheriff, who grunted but offered no other greeting. Lex wanted to ask a few questions, but decided to wait until they reached Beaver Fork. The creek was three miles from town, and Lex could see the scattered cottonwoods lining its bank. When they were within half a mile, three tiny figures could be seen huddled together under one of the taller trees, and Harkness pushed his mount a little harder.

Lex stayed right with him. The three figures slowly resolved themselves into three cowhands. Their horses were nearby, a dark smear against the trees. Harkness skidded to a halt, so close to the hands that his horse's hooves scattered dirt and pebbles on their boots.

"All right," he said, "what the hell's going on here?"

"See for yourself, Roy," one of the hands said, gesturing with one gloved hand. "Down by the water."

Lex dismounted and fell in behind the taller sheriff, who stomped through the sparse undergrowth until he reached the creek bank. Lex could see the bodies now, over Harkness's shoulder. Two men, their hands bound behind them, swung gently from side to side. The thick ropes around their necks looked almost like scarves. The stench of voided bowels clung to the weeds and leaves of the cottonwoods.

"Wasn't too long ago, by the smell of it," Harkness grunted.

"You know them, sheriff?" Lex asked.

"Course I do. Soon's I see their faces, I'll tell you who they were. I know everybody in the damn county, Cranshaw. That's why you got no damn business here."

Lex moved carefully around the dangling forms. "Jesus Christ," he said, turning away.

"What's the matter, Cranshaw? No stomach for your work?" Harkness joined him, then suppressed a gag. "God in heaven!"

Lex shook his head. "That's a new wrinkle, isn't it, Harkness?"

The sheriff glared at him, balled both his fists, then let his hands fall to his sides. The fingers continued to clench and unclench for a moment, as if they had lives of their own. "Who in hell would do something like that?"

"It's your county, sheriff."

Lex stepped closer, trying to blot out the smell. And under the stench was another, more sickening odor. It was the smell of burned meat or, more precisely, flesh. Both men had a brand etched deeply into their foreheads. Lex had seen the brand before. It was that same Rocking U, this time as perfect as it could have been.

"Whose brand is that, Harkness?"

The sheriff whirled around. "Damn you, Cranshaw, mind your own business, I told you. I'll handle this."

"You're not doing too well so far."

"Don't stick your nose in where it don't belong."

"I asked you who used that brand."

"And I told you to mind your own damn business." Harkness pulled his gun suddenly, leveled it at Lex and called to the hands who were hanging back beyond the undergrowth. "Ricky, git on in here."

"I already seen it, sheriff. Don't care to see it again, if you don't mind."

"Damn it, Ricky, I told you to come here."

The cowhand grumbled as he floundered through the brush. He stopped with his mouth open when he saw the pistol in the sheriff's hand.

"Don't stand there gawkin', Ricky. I want you to take Mr. Cranshaw back to town. Pronto!"

"But sheriff, I . . . "

"You gonna do it or am I gonna have to get someone to run you in, too?"

"I'll do it, I'll do it, but . . . "

"Now, Ricky!"

Ricky looked at Cranshaw, shrugged to indicate his helplessness, and drew his gun. "Sorry about this, Cranshaw."

"Sorry my ass," Harkness barked. "You don't have to apologize to him. You just do like I tell you. Take him back to town and put him in a cell until I get there. And I want you to stay put, too. Keep an eye on him."

Harkness reached over, pulled Cranshaw's gun and jammed it into his belt. "You'll get this back when I'm ready to give it to you," he said.

Ricky waved his Colt, and Lex stepped toward the brush.

"Ricky," Harkness said, "he gives you any trouble, you have my permission to blow his sorry ass right out of the saddle. You hear?"

"I heard you, Roy."

The other hands looked confused when Lex stepped into the clear, Ricky a few paces behind him. They started to ask what was going on, but Ricky shook his head and cocked a thumb over his shoulder. "Ask Roy," he said, "'cause I sure as hell don't know."

He waited for Lex to mount up, then climbed into his own saddle. "You stay a few yards in front of me, Cranshaw. You heard what the sheriff said. I don't want to have to shoot you, but I swear to God, I will if you give me cause."

They had gone half a mile when Lex turned and said, "Whose brand is that, Ricky?"

"I can't tell you nothing. You know that."

"I'll find out anyhow, Ricky."

Ricky didn't say anything, and Lex dropped it. They rode the rest of the way in silence. As they entered Carney, a small crowd gathered behind them, and had grown to twenty-five or thirty by the time they reined in in front of the sheriff's office.

Ricky shook off their questions and led Lex inside. He put him in a small cell, turned the key in the lock, and tucked the key into his pocket.

"You never heard this from me," he said suddenly.

"Heard what?"

"That brand?" he leaned closer and cupped one hand around his whisper. "It's registered to Isaac Otterkill."

T was sundown by the time Harkness finally returned. He was curiously subdued, so unlike his morning belligerence, as he walked into the cellblock of the Carney jail. The key to Cranshaw's cell dangled from one hand. He stared absently at the key as he stopped in front of the cell door. Lex waited patiently, but Harkness seemed to be in no hurry to cut him loose. A cigarette drooped from one corner of the sheriff's mouth, and a thin trickle of smoke curled around the brim of his hat.

Finally, he looked at Lex, sucked the last smoke from the butt and dropped it on the floor. Staring down at his boot, Harkness ground the butt under his heel with more viciousness than a man usually wasted on a cigarette. He looked more like a man killing a noxious insect.

Still looking at the floor, he finally spoke. "That was about the ugliest thing I ever seen, Cranshaw. I don't mind telling you, I wanted to puke."

"Why in hell won't you let me help put a stop to it, sheriff?"

"A man's work is all he is, Cranshaw. You can understand that, can't you? Folks around here pay me to look after them. I can't do it, I shouldn't be taking their money."

"That's crazy, sheriff. Nobody expects you to be perfect."

"I do, Cranshaw. I do expect that. I always do my job, always have and always will."

"And if the job is too big for you?"

Harkness snapped his head up as if he'd been clipped on the chin. "You sayin' I ain't up to it?"

"No. Just that maybe you need some help, that's all."

"I need help, I'll tell you. Until then, I want you to butt out. 'Fore I open this cell, I want your word on that."

"You might as well swallow the key, sheriff."

"You are one stubborn bastard. But then, I guess you guys are famous for that, aren't you? My daddy rode with Captain Hays. You know that?"

"No. I never met Hays."

"Toughest sumbitch ever put on pants, the way my daddy used to tell it."

"So I heard."

"How about you, Cranshaw. You tough?"

"I'm not the one to judge that, sheriff."

"You are though, aren't you. I can see it. You got them cold eyes, like a snake's. Little blue-green marbles. They shine but they ain't at all warm. Inhuman, almost. Like my daddy's eyes." He turned his back and walked to the office door. He stopped with one hand on the doorjamb. The keys bounced on his palm as if he were trying to guess their weight. His head bobbed once, then again, and he turned back. Without a word, he jabbed the key into the lock, ground it open and stepped back. "Come on, damn you, git on out of there."

Lex pushed the door open and stepped out of the cell. Harkness walked into the outer office and dropped heavily into his chair. He propped his feet up on the desk and jabbed his chin toward an empty chair. "Sit down," he said.

Pulling the chair close to the front of the desk, Lex lowered himself cautiously to the seat. Harkness opened a drawer in the desk, pulled Lex's gun out and set it on the desk. "You'll be needing that, I reckon."

"I thank you." Lex leaned forward, took the gun and cracked it open. Satisfied that it was loaded, he dropped it into his holster.

"You're not going to go away, no matter how hard I wish, are you?" Harkness seemed somehow saddened by the thought. He watched Lex closely, and smiled when Lex nodded. "I didn't think so."

"You going to let me help?"

Harkness licked his lower lip. The sound was like the rustle of fine paper. "Yeah, yeah I am."

"I know it's not an easy thing for you to do, sheriff."

"Hell, Cranshaw, it was easy, they wouldn't call it work, would they?"

"What started this mess?"

"Nobody knows, at least, not that they're saying. The first one, Timmy Carter, was a drifter. Hell, it took me a week to find out his name. He'd been around a few weeks, but nobody knew what the hell he did. Didn't work for nobody, so folks assumed he was up to no good. Can't blame them for that, I guess. But yet and still, nobody ever accused him of nothing. To this day, I don't know who hung him or why. After a month, I figured it was just one of them things. Maybe he crossed somebody, maybe somebody with a grudge tracked him down from somewhere else."

"Ever hear stories about him?"

"Nothing. Then the cows started disappearing. It wasn't much at first. Just a few head, strays mostly. So nobody was even sure they was missing. Until Steve Holliman found a bunch of his cows penned up in a box canyon about ten miles south of here. They was his, he could tell by the brand, and there wasn't no other marks on 'em, but somebody had rounded them up sure enough, and it didn't take no scientist to guess what they was in that canyon for."

"Tell me about Holliman."

"What's to tell? The usual thing. He come up the hard way. After the war, he drifted down here from someplace in Tennessee. Drove a couple of herds up to Kansas and plowed the money into land. Now he owns half the county and probably half the cows in it."

"Where does Billy Otterkill fit in?"

"He don't. That's what makes the whole thing so damn frustrating. Anyhow, the second hangin' was a couple

THE RANGER ★ 59

days after Steve run across them cows. There didn't
seem to be any connection, but you got to figure there
must be. No connection between Carter and the second
one, a fella name of Johnson. No connection between
Johnson and them cows. But there's got to be."

"How about Otterkill?"

"Billy was all right, as far as I knew. Never heard nothing
bad about him. Then folks started sayin' he was rustling.
Said it was him penned Holliman's steers. After awhile,
everybody, I guess me included, started believing it. I
wanted to believe it, because it made it easier, you know?
I mean, I didn't know nothing bad about him. But there
was that branding iron under the tree they hung him
from. So we all just started pretending like he deserved
to be hung. Didn't take long, neither. Not after the first
two. Seems like it's been goin' on forever, now."

"What brand was the iron?"

"Rocking U. Isaac Otterkill's brand, but it wasn't a regular iron. The u was wider than usual. Nobody thought
much of it, but it seemed kind of strange. Isaac claimed
he never saw it before, that it wasn't his and it wasn't
Billy's."

"Why did Isaac leave him hanging there? Why did you,
for that matter?"

"Isaac's kind of funny. He said he wanted Billy left there
until the man who hung him was hanged right alongside
Billy. Folks didn't like it, I know I sure didn't, but then
Holliman said Billy was stealin' his cows and he'd hang
anybody tried to cut Billy down. Including me."

"You afraid of Holliman?"

Harkness didn't answer right away. Instead, he leaned back in his chair, pulled his pouch out of his pocket and rolled a cigarette. The sheriff paid very careful attention to his tobacco and played with the paper awhile, trying to frame his answer. When he was ready, he stuck the cigarette between his dry lips and lit it. Around the end of the cigarette, he puffed the words out along with the first smoke. "I wouldn't say scared, exactly. But Steve Holliman is a powerful man. And he's got some on his payroll wouldn't blink at killing a baby, let alone a lawman. Since Isaac didn't want Billy cut down, and Holliman didn't either, I just figured there was no point in getting them both mad."

"Who were those men killed today? They connected to the others, or to Billy Otterkill?"

"Now that's the damndest thing, Cranshaw. Them two work for Holliman. Or they did, anyhow. And that tells me who strung them up."

"Isaac Otterkill." It wasn't a question, and Harkness knew it.

"Who else coulda done it?"

"But why?"

"Isaac ain't all there, Cranshaw. You got to understand that. He's half-crazy some time and flat-out crazy the rest of the time. I figure he must have blamed Holliman for what happened to Billy. Probably figures he'll get even this way. Only he ain't counting on Holliman fighting back. Which he will as sure as I got a nose on my face."

"So let's go."

"Where?"

"To arrest Isaac Otterkill."

"Didn't you hear me? I just told you the old man's a lunatic. No way in hell I'm going out there after dark. I wear a necktie, I want my wife to pick it out for me, not some loony old man."

"You think Holliman will wait till morning?"

"If he don't, the way I figure it, he'll just save the county the cost of a trial. That's a bargain."

"You don't mean that."

Harkness sighed. "Yeah, I do, but you're right. We got to go get him."

"And there's something you might have overlooked."

"What's that?"

"Maybe Isaac didn't do it."

Harkness laughed. It was a deep and surprisingly pleasant sound. "This ain't Austin, Mr. Cranshaw. This is the real world. Out here, a man's got a reason to do something, and that thing gets done, you can damn sure bet your horse he done it. Not nobody else."

"Why would Isaac practically leave a confession, if that's what those brands were supposed to be? It doesn't make any sense."

"I already told you. He's crazy. You can't expect a crazy man to make sense. He don't have to. Hell, he ain't supposed to. He makes sense, then he ain't crazy. And who but a crazy man would hang two men and brand them first? You think a sane man would do that?"

Lex thought about it for a moment, There was another answer than the one Harkness expected, but he had no support for it. Yet. But he'd be willing to bet it was out there somewhere. All he had to do was buy himself enough time, and figure out where to look. Isaac Otterkill might be an eccentric. He might even be as crazy as Harkness thought he was, but Isaac was not a fool.

But Lex knew that the minute Isaac was dead, the whole episode would be forgotten. Nobody wanted to think about it, nobody wanted to talk about it. The town wanted it all swept under a rug, the sooner the better. But there was more to this than met the eye.

The more it looked like a simple matter of rustling and vengeance for vigilante justice, the more certain Lex became that someone was doing his damndest to make muddy waters look cleaner than they were. Arresting Isaac Otterkill would do two things—it would protect the old man from whoever wanted him dead, and it would suggest to that same someone that his plan was working. Presuming all the while, of course, that Harkness was wrong, that Isaac wasn't just some crazy man luna- tic enough to hang somebody and then leave all the signs anybody would ever need pointing right to his front door.

But Harkness was wrong. He just had to be. Isaac wasn't that crazy, Lex thought, if he's crazy at all. The trouble with that idea was it left Lex out in the cold with a couple of very difficult questions—if Isaac didn't hang the two men that morning, who did?

And why?

LEX returned to his room more confused than ever. He lit the coal-oil lamp and lay down on the bed without taking off his boots or his gun. He stared at the ceiling, tracing a fine network of cracks. Like a child seeing monsters in the clouds, he imagined one grotesque figure after another in the thin lines. Each time he tried to focus on one, to bring it into the foreground, it would change shape on him and fade away, only to be replaced by another.

He closed his eyes, feeling a wave of exhaustion sweep over him, but he fought against the desire to sleep. He had too much to sort out. He had a fistful of pieces and he wasn't even sure they all belonged to the same puzzle. If only he knew who had sent the letter to Austin, he'd have someplace to start that made sense.

Forcing his eyes open again, he threw his legs over

the side of the bed and let his feet touch the floor. His portmanteau was in the corner, and he stared at it for some time, knowing he was going to read the letter again, and knowing, too, that when he had finished it, he would know no more than he knew before.

Like a man who can't keep from picking at a scab, he got up and walked to the bag in the corner. He picked it up, set it in on the dresser and opened it. In a small pocket sewn into one side of the lining was the letter. He pulled it out, opened the envelope and removed the cryptic note, leaving the envelope on the dresser. Lex backed toward the bed until his legs hit the edge of the mattress, then he sat down without looking.

Unfolding the single piece of cheap paper, he read the note for what must have been the hundredth time. The paper looked as if it had been torn from a notebook of some kind, a school tablet or something of the kind. Other than that, there was nothing unusual or distinctive about it.

they's hangin folks, but it ain't what it looks to be. send somebody 2 Carney quic. Billy ain't done nothin'. neethur did the others. there wil be mor les you send somebody quik.

It was unsigned and undated. All he could tell for certain was that it must have been written shortly after Billy Otterkill was hanged. That, and that whoever wrote the letter knew something Lex needed to know.

He folded the paper and leaned back on the bed again. There was no way to trace the author, because it had been hand-delivered. No one in Austin knew who had brought it, and there was no sure way to track it back to Carney and the hand of its writer. Lex had to hope that whoever it was would get in touch with him. But he'd already been in Carney for two days, and there was no indication that would happen anytime soon. If the writer of the note were waiting to work up his courage, it was taking him an awful long time.

Bone tired, Lex stood up just long enough to pull the quilt down and collapsed on the mattress again, leaned over to pull off his boots, then unbuckled his gunbelt and set it on the floor beside the bed. Lying back, he closed his eyes again, but he couldn't get comfortable. He was not used to comfort, and realized the pillow was too soft. Lex swept it off the bed without looking, then let his head fall back. He felt something sharp dig into his neck, thought it might be a bug and brushed his hand under his head when he felt something with his fingers.

It was another envelope. This one had no address, but it was the same cheap paper. He cursed under his breath as he tore it open. Inside, another sheet of paper, a simple brown wrapping paper, this one just as nondescript as the first, had been folded twice. He opened it, aware that his hands were trembling slightly.

There, in the same ragged scrawl, was another message:

Isak's boys din't steal no cows

Lex knew immediately that the writer must know who did steal the cattle Holliman found penned in the box canyon. But how?

He knew there was no sleeping now. He reached down

and snagged his gunbelt, buckled it on and walked down-stairs to the front door in his stockinged feet. Lex walked out onto the porch and sat on the top step. Rolling a ciga-rette, he listened to the crickets, and off in the distance, an owl screeching as it swept low across the barren fields.

The sky was a blue so dark it was almost pitch-black, and the stars winked on and off like semaphores, in a code he couldn't read, sending him a message he couldn't understand. He pulled out his pocket watch. In the glow of the cigarette, he read the time — ten-thirty.

It was going to be a long night. When the cigarette was finished, he flicked it away and started rolling a sec-ond.

"Mr. Cranshaw? Anything wrong?" The door opened behind him and Elizabeth Helderson stepped onto the porch. "I heard you come out. I hope you don't mind . . ."

"No, not at all."

She sat in a swing off to one side. He thought she was going to bore him with idle chatter, but she sat quietly. After a couple of minutes, she started to hum. He felt as if he ought to be sociable, but didn't really know how. He wasn't used to women, and he wasn't used to talking unless he had something specific to say, and even then he used as few words as he could manage.

Lex puffed on the cigarette, leaning back against a pil-lar. Finally, after a long exhale, he said, "Did anyone come to see me today?"

"Why, no. Were you expecting someone?"

"No."

"I see. Then you always ask whether someone you

weren't expecting paid a visit you were not anticipating, is that it?"

Lex didn't answer. He could hear the mocking edge to her voice, and it threw him off balance. He sensed that he could trust her, but that, too, was something he was not used to doing. He debated for a long moment whether or not to tell her about the note. Deciding he had nothing to lose, he cleared his throat and turned to face her. In the shadows under the porch roof, he could barely make out her form huddled on the swing. "I found an envelope under my pillow," he said.

"And you think I put it there?"

"I don't know what to think. I thought maybe someone delivered it for me."

"No. Nothing like that happened."

"Was there anyone in the house at all?"

"Mr. Carson and Mr. Tunney. No one out of the ordinary. And your room was locked, as usual."

"I see."

"What was in the envelope?"

"Nothing much."

Again, that mocking edge crept into her voice. "So you want to know who you should thank . . . "

"I want to know where the goddamned letter came from. I want to know who sent it. That's what I want to know."

He thought the profanity might shock her into an admission, but her voice was unruffled as before. "I'm afraid I can't help you. There was just myself and Beatrice. No one else."

"Beatrice?"

"Beatrice Macready. My housekeeper . . . but I'm sure she'd have told me if someone had delivered a letter for you."

"Maybe she wrote it herself."

"Not likely. She doesn't read or write very well at all."

"Can you ask her about it for me?"

"If you like . . . "

"I'd like."

"Very well, then. Tomorrow. Unless you want to roust the poor woman out of bed in the middle of the night. You don't want to do that, do you?"

"Look, I'm sorry to seem so . . . impatient. But . . . "

"I understand, Mr. Cranshaw. I know you have a serious problem to deal with, but I don't see how Beatrice could be involved."

"I don't know that she is. But somebody put that letter in my room. And I have to find out who. And why."

Elizabeth hummed a little louder, the soft lilt punctuated by the creak of the swing. "Good night, then, Mr. Cranshaw. I'll speak to Beatrice in the morning."

"I'd rather do that myself, if you don't mind."

"Very well. But I insist on being present. I don't want you intimidating the poor woman."

"Do I seem like the sort of man who . . . never mind."

Lex stood and watched his hostess slide from the swing and move toward the door. The limp was barely noticeable in the dark, but he could hear the unevenness of her steps on the painted wood. When she was gone, he waited a decent interval, then went inside himself. He locked the door and climbed the stairs slowly. Once in his room, he sat on the bed again to re-read the note. It still told him nothing useful. Reluctantly, he folded the paper and walked to the dresser, where he slipped it back into the envelope and put it in his portmanteau with the original letter.

Back at the bed, he sat for a moment, then reached for the lamp. Just as his fingers grasped the wick turn, the lamp shattered. The fuel began to spread in a flaming puddle on the floor as the sound of a distant crack registered dimly.

Lex snatched the quilt and began to beat the flames, then realizing he was just spreading the blaze, he spread the fabric over the puddled flames and yanked the mattress off the bed frame. Much of the fire was already smothered and the dull orange glow had all but disappeared. As he dumped the mattress on top of the quilt, the window blew out, and shards of glass nicked his hands and face.

Lex dove to the floor, knowing that it was wasted effort. The bullet was already buried in the wall behind him. He lay there on the floor, breathing in the acrid fumes of the coal oil and the sharp tang of scorched cloth and seared feathers from the quilt.

It took a moment for the sharp rapping on his door to register.

"Mr. Cranshaw, Mr. Cranshaw, are you all right? What's going on?"

"I'm all right," Lex said, scrambling to his feet and moving toward the door.

When he yanked it open, he could see Tunney and Carson, the latter in a nightcap, craning their necks to see into the room. Behind them, holding a lamp above her head, Elizabeth Helderson was trying to get past. "Are you all right, Mr. Cranshaw?" she asked.

He nodded.

Lex got a whiff of the smoke as it swirled past him and out the door. Elizabeth seemed to notice it at the same time. One hand went to her mouth and she chewed on her knuckles a moment. Then, the hand still in front of her mouth, she asked, "What happened? I smell smoke. Is there a fire? Is something burning?"

She pushed between her boarders and stepped into the room. Holding the lamp before her as if to ward off something terrible she feared she might see, she moved toward the bed. It was impossible to miss the wreckage beside the now-vacant bedframe. Lex grabbed her by the arm and pulled her back toward the doorway.

"Let me go," she snapped, jerking her arm from his grasp.

"You can't bring that lamp in here," Lex said.

"What did you do to the bed?"

"I didn't do anything. Someone tried to kill me. A gunshot broke the lamp and started a fire. I put it out. Now please, just stay away from the window with the light. Whoever shot at me may still be out there."

"This won't do, Mr. Cranshaw," she said.

Lex nodded. "Damn right it won't," he muttered.

LEX stayed up all night. It was pointless to go looking for the sniper, but he couldn't risk sleep, not when someone was within a few hundred yards of the house, someone with a buffalo gun and the intention to commit murder. He stayed in the dark, sometimes lying on the settee in the parlor and sometimes pacing the floor, arms behind his back like an angry schoolmaster.

Every fifteen or twenty minutes he would walk to the window and look out, wondering where the hell the sun was and why it was taking so damn long to come up. By five o'clock, the sky finally started to brighten, but it still wasn't enough for Lex. He stared at the gray blur around the curtain, chewing on his lip and counting the seconds.

He was supposed to meet Harkness at six-thirty. That

would be the beginning. Now that the sheriff had swallowed his pride, or his fear of Steve Holliman or whatever else had hogtied him, they could make some progress. And Lex was determined to put an end to the creeping madness that was eating at the town like some invisible worm.

Elizabeth came down at five-thirty. It was obvious she hadn't slept either. She wanted to put up coffee. Lex went to the well, carrying a pail for fresh water in his left hand and his Colt in his right. He kept his thumb on the hammer, and cranked the pail down and back with his left hand. His eyes never stopped moving, and he felt the hair on the back of his neck standing on end.

He carried the pail back to the kitchen, stopping once more to stare out at the deserted flats beyond the house. Lex stayed in the kitchen with Elizabeth, making sure the curtains were drawn and trying to listen to the growing clamor of the morning over the clatter of utensils. She said nothing, but he knew she was angry at him. He also knew she was only too aware that she had no reason to be. But her house had almost been set ablaze, and she had to direct her anger and her fear at someone. Lex would have to do. And he could live with it.

When the coffee was on the wood stove, Elizabeth sat across from him at a round table. Her hands were restless, the fingers twitching, sometimes getting tangled in themselves, sometimes dragging the hands across the smooth wood like spiders.

The coffee started to to burble in the pot. So far, she hadn't said a word. Lex wanted to say something to reassure her, but knew there was nothing he *could* say. When the coffee was done, she got up and poured them each a cup without looking at him. She shoved his mug across the table, then lowered herself slowly to the chair.

He took a sip, ignoring the searing heat. Setting the cup carefully on the table, he said, "I'll be moving out, of course."

"Of course."

"I want you to make sure everybody knows it. That way you'll be safe."

"Of course. Safe. In my own home. The way I ought to be."

She sipped her own coffee. Holding the mug, she peered at him from behind it. "You don't know who's doing all these terrible things, do you?"

Lex shook his head. "But somebody does," he said. "And that somebody thinks I can find out. And I will do just that."

Lex took a long swallow of the coffee, gulping the hot liquid as if it were some trial by fire. He set the mug down with a sharp crack. "I'll be back this afternoon, to talk to your friend, Beatrice."

"I'd rather you didn't come back. I'm sorry. But I'll tell you where to find her. You can go there. I'll tell her to expect you."

"All right. I understand."

"I don't care whether you understand or not. I want this to stop. I want it to stop now, and I don't care what has to be done to stop it. Just do it."

She got up and went into the parlor. Lex finished his coffee. As he put the empty mug down, Elizabeth came back into the kitchen. She held a sheet of paper, folded once, in her trembling hands. Setting it down across from him, leaning forward as if she didn't want to get too close, she said, "Here are the directions." She turned and was gone.

And Lex knew she wasn't coming back. Not until he was packed and gone.

He tucked the paper into his pocket and left the kitchen. He didn't expect her to be in the parlor. She wasn't. Climbing the stairs slowly, he went to his former room and packed his few things in the leather portmanteau. When he was finished, he looked at the charred mess on the floor, then at the shattered window, the curtains torn aside, shards of glass glittering in the morning sunlight on the floor, and shook his head.

He moved quickly now, and descended the stairs two at a time. He went to the barn and saddled his horse, then led it outside. He looked at the house for a moment. For a second, he caught a glimpse of Elizabeth Helderson through the shattered window. She ripped the dangling curtains down and rolled them into a ball. She stopped for a moment, as if she felt his eyes on her, then looked toward the open door of the barn. If she saw him standing there, she made no sign. A moment later, the window was empty.

He still had half an hour. Taking a line from the window, he rode out a hundred yards or so, then dismounted. Lex tethered his mount to a scrub oak and walked in alternating arcs, slowly moving farther and farther away from the house. He didn't know what he was looking for, didn't know if he would find anything at all. But it was better than letting the impatience tear at his gut any longer.

There was little cover. But the gunman didn't need cover, not for a long shot in the middle of the night. All he needed was a place to stand within plain sight of the Helderson house. The bullet that shattered the lamp had come through the center of the window. Its path gave him a rough idea of the shooter's angle, but not the distance. A Sharps, in the right hands, was accurate up to nearly a thousand yards. Some said even longer if the shooter was good. The longer the shot, the wider the arc he had to walk.

At six hundred yards, he found tracks in the dust. The ground was so dry it was difficult to tell whether they were fresh or not. He followed them for fifty yards, leaning close to the ground to keep from losing them. There was a trampled spot and a couple of horse apples. From the look of them, they couldn't be more than a few hours old.

Heading away from the trampled spot in the dust, two sets of boot prints, each pointing opposite the other, led him to a clump of stunted brush, hard against a long, flat slab of rock. Someone had walked toward the rock and then back. The prints disappeared then, and Lex circled the slab slowly, careful not to disturb the ground, making sure there was nothing of interest before he took each step.

Whoever had made the prints had walked to the stone, climbed up on it, then walked back the way he had come.

Lex climbed up on the slab himself. He looked toward the house, already knowing that it was a perfect location from which to fire the bullets that had ripped into his room the night before. But knowing it and proving it were two different things. And proving who had done it was so far beyond his reach at the moment that he didn't even let himself dwell on it.

He lay on the rock, mimed aiming a rifle. He had to shift his body to avoid some of the brush, rolled to his left, then to his right, looking for the perfect place. When he found the clearest shot, he crawled forward and looked down into the dry and brittle brush. This time, he knew what he was looking for. It took him a while, but he found it, just as he knew he would. An empty cartridge lay on its side in the sand against the front edge of the slab.

He leaned down, almost losing his balance, and managed to grab the cartridge casing. Thorns ripped at the back of his hand as he pulled the empty shell out of the brush. It was identical to the one he'd found the day before. It didn't help much, but at least he knew it was the same man, stalking him from place to place. He was being hunted by a man who had known why he had come to Carney. That could only mean the hunter also knew about the hangings, and was determined that he would not live to do anything about them.

But why?

Lex was pleased to find another piece of the puzzle, and angry that it explained nothing. He sat on the rock looking toward the house, tucked the shell into his pocket, and finally climbed down. He started toward his horse, broke into a sprint, and realized he was running because he didn't know what else to do. The uncertainty was eating him up.

Lex rode toward town, rolling the puzzle pieces over and over in his mind. Each was becoming smooth, like gemstones polished in a tumbler. And the smoother they became, the harder it was to see how they fit together, or if they fit at all.

As he entered the town, he could see the sheriff's horse in front of his office. At least that part of it was going according to plan. It was a relief to know that something worked as it was supposed to.

Carney was stone quiet. The clop of his horse's hooves echoed dully off the bleached wooden walls of the shops and saloons. Carney was on the edge of becoming a ghost town, and didn't know it. This is what it would be like when everyone was gone. The same ugly storefronts, the same dirty windows. The same quiet. This was a dress rehearsal for oblivion.

When he dismounted in front of the sheriff's office, he paused to look up the street in each direction. Lex scanned the roofs of the buildings across the street, half expecting to see the octagonal barrel of a Sharps pointing at him like a skeletal finger. But the roofs were as dead and empty as the streets.

The door was closed, and he rapped on it, rattling the glass. There was no answer, so he tried the knob. The door was unlocked, and he opened it slowly. He looked at the desk, thinking maybe Harkness had fallen asleep.

When he stepped inside, the office was deserted.

"Sheriff?"

No answer.

"Sheriff Harkness? You there?"

Quiet.

Lex went back outside and stood on the wooden walkway. Looking up and down the street, he still saw nothing. None of the stores or saloons was open. There was only one restaurant, on the ground floor of the Hotel Carney. Maybe Harkness was getting something to eat. He stepped down into the street and headed up the block to the hotel.

When he stepped inside, two men were seated, at separate tables. He asked a waitress if Harkness had been in, and she shook her head. "Haven't seen him," she said. "Not since he rode in, about an hour ago. He's in his office, I expect."

Lex thanked her and walked back to the office. The front office was just as deserted. He looked at the door to the cellblock, and his spine turned to ice.

Pulling his Colt, he walked to the door and looked through the metal grate. It was dark in the cellblock and he could only see two of the three cells. The key dangled from the lock and he turned it, then pulled the door open. The hinges creaked and the door bumped the wall with a dull thump that echoed from the cellblock.

The two cells he'd seen were full of shadow. The third, the only one with a window, was better lit. A square beam of sunlight angled across the cell. Dead center, like a star in a spotlight,. was Roy Harkness, hanging from the ceiling.

10

LEX cut Roy Harkness down, and lay the sheriff's body on a straw-filled pallet in one corner of the cell. The initial shock behind him now, he saw the bullet hole in the sheriff's back. This time, it seemed the hangman had to kill his victim first. The hanging was an afterthought. But analysis could wait until later. Leaving the cell door open, Lex walked out of the block, closed the door and locked it. Tucking the key in his pocket, he sprinted up the block, back to the restaurant.

The waitress gaped in astonishment when he burst through the double glass doors. "Does the sheriff have a deputy?" he asked.

One hand went to her mouth and she seemed frozen. Her jaw went slack, then she tried to talk, managing only a stammer.

"Does he, damn it? Tell me!"

The cook heard the commotion and came out of the kitchen. In one hand he carried a cleaver and he stared at Lex uneasily. "What's the trouble here? You all right, Rose?" He tugged at the waitress, pulling her behind him, then backing up a step.

"Does the sheriff have a deputy?" Lex repeated.

"Yeah. Roy's nephew works with him, why?"

Lex took a step forward, reaching for the key. The cook backed up another step, watching the hand until it reappeared with the key. "Here, take this." Lex thrust the key toward the retreating cook, who had no choice but to reach out and take it.

"What's going on, dammit?" the cook snapped.

Lex pointed toward the waitress with his chin. The cook seemed confused for a second, then, when he understood what Lex wanted, he turned to the waitress. "Rose, you go on in back, honey. I'll be in in a minute."

Only too glad to comply, Rose disappeared into the kitchen. Quickly, Lex explained what had happened. "You get the deputy, tell him what happened. Maybe you better get somebody to go with you, since they're kin."

"Then what?"

Lex threw his hands wide. "I don't know. I can't worry about that now. I'll be back as soon as I can."

"Where you going?"

"I want to talk to Isaac Otterkill."

The cook nodded almost as if he'd suspected as much. Lex turned and sprinted back into the street, picking up speed as he approached the sheriff's office. He was in the saddle in an instant, and kicked his mount unmercifully as he raced toward the edge of town.

He broke into the flats at a full gallop, knowing that he might be taking on more than he could handle, but knowing too, he had no choice. If Isaac Otterkill was responsible for the hanging, he'd be expecting trouble. Unless he was as crazy as everyone seemed to think.

All the way out, Lex kept whipping himself. There had been three men hanged before he got to Carney. And three since. A fat lot of good he'd done. Deep down, he accused himself. There had to be something he should have done, some little thing he'd overlooked. But he'd thought it through again and again. Step by step he worked it out one more time. And always, he kept coming back to the note. Maybe that was it. Maybe the writer did know something. But he didn't even know for sure who the writer was.

And he had to ask himself whether Harkness would still be alive if he hadn't twisted the sheriff's arm and forced him to open up. But if there was a connection, then the killer or killers had to be in a position to know about it. Who had Harkness talked to?

Another piece, or another puzzle? Lex wanted to scream. He wanted to pull his Colt and shoot the sky full of holes until the truth came leaking down, drop by bloody drop. He felt as if he were losing control, like everything around him was moving faster and faster, and he couldn't move his feet fast enough to keep his balance.

As he drew closer to the Otterkill's ranch, he slowed his mount. Part of him wanted to barrel in under a full head of steam, but there was no point in putting his own neck in a noose. With a mile still to go, he slowed his roan to a walk. Out of the corner of his eye, he noticed some steers, and he nudged his mount in their direction, getting close enough to check the brands. They all carried the Rocking U, but it looked somehow different. He couldn't put his finger on it at first, and he wanted to get even closer. He cut one of the smaller steers out of the herd, then put a rope on the frightened animal.

The others bolted, and he watched them race off into the flat wasteland, a small cloud of dust boiling up behind them. He regretted the noise, but there was nothing to be done about it. Tightening the rope, he looped it over his saddle horn and sprang from the saddle, grabbing the line with one gloved hand as he moved in on the kicking animal.

Lex could see the brand more clearly now, and it still didn't look the same as the ones he'd seen before. Then it hit him. This *U* was narrower. It was just as tall as the other, but the distance between the upright legs was probably fifty percent smaller.

On a hunch, he tugged the rope harder and got within a couple of feet of the steer's head. The long horns arced toward him as the steer slashed and whipped its head back and forth. Grabbing one horn on its next pass, he twisted, dogging the steer to its knees then onto its side. He checked the earmark now, and saw what he'd expected. The same double cut. But this time there appeared to be no difference in age. Both cuts had been made at the same time, as nearly as he could tell.

That cemented one piece in place. Someone was double cutting the ears of stolen cattle, making a second cut to simulate Otterkill's brand. And the Rocking U was being burned in over another brand, but he didn't know which one. Figure that out, and he knew he'd have a lead to Billy Otterkill's hangman. And he hoped to God there was only one.

He loosened the rope and jumped clear as the steer climbed to its feet, turned on him and pawed the ground. He thought for a second the steer was going to charge, and he took off his hat and flapped it against his thigh. The steer backed away a step, then another, then, tossing its ugly horns once more, turned and galloped after the others, now a small, milling knot a half-mile away.

He could just make out the roof of the Otterkill place now through the shimmering haze as the sun started to climb higher and the ground began to heat up. The heated air curled and boiled, distorting everything as it bent the light.

This time, Lex was determined to arrive both unannounced and prepared. He walked back to his horse, coiling the rope with both hands, secured it on his saddle, and jerked his Winchester from its boot.

He grabbed the reins to his horse, then jerked a shell into the Winchester's chamber and cocked the hammer. It would take him a good half-hour to work his way around along the Otterkill spread, and slip in behind the house. But if he expected to get anywhere, and keep himself alive long enough to do it, he was going to have to expect the worst.

The creek that cut in behind Isaac's spread was off to his left, a quarter-mile away. Its ragged brush and scattered trees weren't much cover, but it was all he had. He tugged the roan after him and, ten minutes later, pulled the horse into a clump of brush, tethered it and started for Otterkill's.

The brush didn't offer much resistance, and he slipped through and out into the ragged grass on the far side of the creek. He broke into a lope, wanting to close the distance quickly, but not leave himself winded when he got close. He was feeling more confident now. Doing something at last, he felt as if he were taking charge again. He lowered the hammer, cursing himself for not doing it sooner, and bent low as he caught a glimpse of the Otterkill house through a small stand of willows.

He couldn't see clearly enough to judge whether anyone was home. The creek was making its curving approach to the rear of the place now, and he slowed to a fast walk, then to an even more measured gait. Glimpses of the house were more frequent now, but he still only saw the place in bits and pieces.

The chimney was not giving off smoke, and he couldn't see the front of the place to tell whether or not horses were hitched to the post. In another minute or so, he could see the corral. A sudden break in brush gave him a clear view of the entire rear of the house. He stopped beside a stunted oak, dropped to one knee, and watched the rear of the weathered building for several minutes.

Checking the sun, he guessed it must be nearly eight, maybe even a few minutes after. It seemed odd for the house to be so quiet so late in the morning. Ducking into a crouch, he sprinted across the gap, got behind some more brush, and moved another fifty yards along the creek.

Lex was directly behind the house. Slipping to the side a couple of feet, he stepped through the undergrowth, reached the creekbank, and stepped into the water. Moving laterally another three yards, he had a clear look at the back wall. A window dead center was half open. Gingham curtains, looking like they were left over from the Polk administration, hung limply on either side. The interior of the house appeared dark, but it might just be in contrast to the bright sun slashing across the weathered, whitened timber of the rear wall.

Planting one foot on the opposite bank, he counted under his breath and launched himself into a sprint on three. He was aware of his feet pounding on the dry earth. Every step sounded like a falling tree to his anxious ears. He cut to the left and covered the last fifty feet before the fence, took the fence on the fly, and crossed the closed-in yard. Lex flattened himself against the wall to the left of the half-open window. His breath came in sharp gasps and he was suddenly aware of his heels sinking into the ground. He looked down and realized he was standing in a freshly planted flower bed.

For a moment, he felt guilty. Then, yanking himself back to the circumstances, knowing that one or more of the men who lived in this house might be responsible for the grotesque death of Roy Harkness, he pushed the budding guilt aside, ripped it up by the roots and tossed it away.

Crouching by the window, he listened for voices, the sound of snoring, maybe the click of a knife on china, even the scrape of a match on a leather heel. But the house was absolutely silent.

Taking off his hat, he leaned closer, then ducked below the sill and slowly came back up, the Winchester in his right hand, cocked again. Lex raised his eyes above the still and peered into the gloom. As nearly as he could tell, which was far from certain, and nowhere near comforting, the room beyond the window was deserted.

Trying the window, he pushed it open even further, holding his breath against the possibility of a creak. The window moved more easily than he had anticipated, and he nearly lost control of it. When he had it open far enough, he stopped to listen one more time then, with a shrug, flung his left leg up and over the sill.

He had the Winchester across his thigh, its muzzle pointed into the room, his wrist bent to keep his finger on the trigger. When no one challenged him, and the first flash of searing pain of a bullet tearing into his flesh failed to materialize, he ducked through, brought his right leg in and found himself standing in a neat bedroom. He started when something moved across the room, then realized he was looking at his own image in a pier glass.

Lex tiptoed to the door, bringing the Winchester around. The room beyond was a sitting room of some sort, more dignified than he would have expected in so rustic a home. There was a bookcase full of leather-backed books, the spines showing the sueding of frequent use.

To the left, sitting with his hat in his lap and a Colt, cocked and ready on the arm of his easy chair, was Isaac Otterkill. Across from him, sitting on the edge of a settee, looking as if she were about to slide off the cushions to the floor, was a young black woman, her hair done in a neat bandanna.

"I think you wanted to talk to Beatrice, Mr. Cranshaw," Isaac said. "Start talking."

11

BEATRICE looked at Lex through hooded eyes. She seemed unsure whether she wanted to smile or to run. Lex guessed she'd prefer the latter. He glanced at Isaac Otterkill, who remained impassive, his right hand resting lightly on the butt of an old Colt Navy pistol. Lex walked toward Beatrice. He sensed that she was frightened, and that with a lawman towering over her, she felt threatened, so he got down on one knee.

"Beatrice," he said.

"Yes, sir."

"I want to ask you a few questions, if you don't mind."

"Yes, sir."

"Don't be afraid. You're not in any trouble. I just want you to tell the truth. All right?"

"Yes, sir."

"Did you write a letter about what happened to Billy Otterkill?"

"No, sir."

"You're sure."

"Yes, sir."

Lex hadn't been prepared for that answer. He looked at Isaac, who nodded his head slightly. Lex took a deep breath. "Do you know who did write the letter?"

"Yes, sir. I do know that."

Swallowing his impatience, Lex shook his head, trying to encourage the young woman. "Who wrote it, Beatrice."

"My mama wrote it. I mean I wrote it down, but she told me what to say. So she wrote it, I guess. And I helped."

"The note at Miss Helderson's boarding house . . . is that from your mother, too?"

This time she just shook her head. Lex looked at Isaac again. The old man was leaning back in his chair, his eyes fixed on Lex, but his face as immobile as a stone mask. It was up to Lex. The next question was the one he needed answered. "Will your mother talk to me? Will she tell me what happened, what she knows, anyway?"

Beatrice shrugged.

"Will you take me to her?" Lex looked at Otterkill again, who was shaking his head no. Beatrice hadn't said anything and Lex turned back, thinking she might have answered him in some other way. He asked again. "Will she see me?"

"I don't know."

"Will you ask her? Please, Beatrice, it's very important."

"Yes, sir, I'll ask her."

Isaac spoke for the first time since the interrogation, such as it was, had begun. His voice seemed to come from some faraway place, as if his body was just a machine through which it passed. "Daniel! Come here, boy."

Lex heard the scrape of a boot on the floor behind him and turned to see Daniel Otterkill, a shotgun draped over his arm, standing in the doorway.

"You take Miss Beatrice to her mama, son. Take Lucas with you. If Mrs. Macready will talk to the ranger, here, you send Lucas on back to fetch him. Make sure you stay there with Mrs. Macready. Understand me, son?"

"Paw, I . . . "

"You do what I say, boy. Things is changed some."

"Yes, Paw."

Beatrice looked at Isaac, her body already beginning to rise, but frozen in that uncertain moment before knowing whether she should. Isaac nodded. It was just the slightest dip of his chin, but Beatrice jumped as if he'd clapped his hands.

Daniel backed through the door and stood aside, the last six inches of the shotgun barrel waving in the emptiness on the other side of the doorway. Beatrice moved quickly, sidestepped the gun barrel, and disappeared. Lex heard footsteps, then the sound of the front door slamming.

"That'd be Daniel," Isaac said. "He doesn't think I ought to be talking to you. He thinks we ought to handle things ourselves. Just like we said we would."

"And what do you think?"

"I think I want the men who killed my Billy feeding

worms. But I think they ought to suffer some, first. The Bible talks about an eye for an eye. I want my eye. So does Daniel. Lucas, too, but he's young yet."

"You knew I'd be coming. Why?"

"I seen the brand on them two boys. I know what it meant. But it don't mean what you're supposed to think."

"You telling me you didn't kill them?"

Isaac didn't answer right away. Lex stared at him, but the old man didn't seem to notice. He could have been alone in the room. His eyes were focused on something far in the distance, out beyond the edge of the world. Lex didn't want to know what he was seeing.

Finally, Isaac picked up the Colt Navy and set it in his lap. "No, I didn't kill them. But I know who did now. Same as I know who killed my Billy. I can't prove it, and neither can you. Not yet. But you got to, and I got to help you."

"Why? Why not just go and do what you want to do? Why not just get even?"

"I'm an old man, Mr. Cranshaw. Things are changing fast, faster all the time. I know that, but I'm too old to change. But my boys, the two I got left . . . they can still change. And I know they got to. I can't stop that. I know that, now. I tried to keep 'em, make 'em be what I was when I was their age. But that was wrong. I see that." He stopped talking, and in the silence, Lex realized he had been listening to history, the past coming to grips with the future.

It was more painful than he had realized. For a man like Isaac Otterkill, rooted so securely in his own past, it must be pure torture. Lex felt like he ought to say something, but he didn't know what to say. In a way, nothing he could say would matter at all to Isaac Otterkill.

The old man sighed. "We got to wait some time. Mrs. Macready lives some ways off."

"You want to tell me what you know while we wait?"

Isaac shook his head. "She'll tell you. You don't need nothing from me. Not yet."

"But I will, is that what you're saying?"

Isaac nodded slowly. "Yes. You will."

Lex didn't push it. He leaned back in his chair, trying to swallow the emotions swirling in his gut every time they tried to climb up and out like some living thing. He listened to the ticking of a grandmother clock on a table in a dark corner of the room. It bonged softly, and he counted to nine. The last chime seemed to fade slowly away, and then the ticking grew louder, filling the space the echo had left behind.

It was near ten when a boot stomped on the front porch. Lex jumped like he'd been shot, then got up and walked toward the front of the house. The door banged back and Lucas Otterkill stood there, a Winchester hanging at his side. Lex noticed the hammer was cocked.

"Mrs. Macready says you should come with me."

Lex turned, expecting Isaac to be right behind him. But the old man was still in the chair in the other room. Lex walked back to the doorway. "You going to come with me?"

"No need. You'll be back here afore long. And I already

know what I need to know. The rest is your business. You do it."

"If that's the way you want it . . . "

"That's the way it has to be."

"Can I ask you one thing?"

Isaac said nothing, and Lex took it as assent. "You know anybody around here shoots a Sharps?"

"Nope."

"You sure? It's important, please think."

"Cranshaw, I know it's important. I told you no. I'll ask around, I see anybody to ask. But that ain't likely."

"How about your boys? Can you have them ask around?"

This time, Lex didn't know what to think of the silence. As it grew longer, he realized he wasn't going to get an answer one way or the other.

He backed out of the room, turned and stepped outside. He let the door close softly. Lucas was already on his mount. He had Lex's horse beside him. When Lex took the reins, Lucas smiled slightly.

"Seen you leave him there," he said. "Good horse."

Lex grunted. Lucas turned without another word, and Lex fell in behind. He wanted to ask how far, but knew Lucas was about as talkative as his father. There was no point. There seemed to be no point to anything about Carney. From the first hanging to the last clatter of the final board falling to the ground when the town was finally gone, there would be no point.

Carney just was. And unless he got a lead soon, it wouldn't be much longer.

It was hard to shake the ice loose from his spine as they rode across the dry, flat land. This part of Texas was so different from the Kentucky of his boyhood. Watching Lucas, not yet out of his teens, bobbing in the saddle ahead of him, he wondered what the kid wanted out of life. He was too young to have been in the war. He had been spared that. But southwest Texas was a lemon from which the last drop of juice had been squeezed.

Lex was from green, rolling country. There were cool breezes, lots of cold, clear streams, trees by the millions. Carney was smack in the middle of hell and almost as hot. It sucked the life out of a man until he was like an empty husk, slowly withering away until one day a hot wind came along and blew him away.

That was what was waiting for Lucas Otterkill. That was what had already dried Isaac into brittle bones and old leather. The strength was still there in the old man, but he must have been like Lucas once. That was a long time ago, so long ago he wondered if Isaac even remembered, or if he could dare to.

Easing his horse up alongside the kid's mount, he caught a glimpse of Lucas, his eyes set dead ahead, his lips a thin white line, as if to protect himself from the desiccating wind, to hang, onto every last drop of vitality and keep himself from becoming a younger version of his father.

That was a hell of a legacy to leave your sons. That had not escaped Isaac's notice, and it seemed to be motivating his change of heart.

The past was such a heavy weight. Even Lex felt his

own, like an anchor strapped to his back with a thousand feet of chain adding to its weight. There was no way to get away from it, not and keep on living.

The young man riding ahead of him should have his whole life to look forward to. But unless Lex got something he could use, and got it soon, the young man might not have a future at all, no matter what Isaac wanted for him.

12

THE tiny cabin was almost hidden by the over-hanging branches of a half-dozen willows. The creek behind the place was wide and sluggish, but it created a broad band of green as it wound its leisurely way across the flatlands. The grass was a little thicker in this valley, as if the soil were more fertile and the climate somehow more hospitable.

As they drew close, Lex let Lucas ease ahead of him a couple of lengths. He could see past the kid to the front porch where Daniel Otterkill sat on the top step with a shotgun across his knees, his elbows braced on the barrel and supporting his head, chin in cupped palms.

As the two men dismounted, Daniel remained motion-less. He didn't acknowledge his brother's hello or Cranshaw's nod, as if he were in a coma, his pale blue eyes flat

97

and unblinking as he stared out into the brilliant sunlight of the late morning.

The house was tidy, and showed those little signs that evidence pride of possession. The window glass was crystal clear, the curtains behind the glass crisp and smooth. The hard-pack dirt before the porch showed signs of having been swept, and the broom that had been used to do it leaned against one corner of the porch railing.

Lucas stepped past Daniel and climbed onto the porch. "Should I take him inside?" Lucas asked. He stared down at the back of his brother's head.

"You should take him out back and put a bullet through his goddamned head. That's what you should do."

"Paw said . . ."

"Paw's going soft in the head. Paw don't have the heart anymore, Luke. He don't want to get even for Billy like he promised. Not anymore, he don't. It's a damn shame."

"But Paw knows what he's doing."

"Paw don't know what day of the week it is, half the time."

Lucas didn't answer right away. He looked at Lex, shrugged his shoulders, then reached down to flick the brim of Daniel's hat with one snapping finger. "Guess I'll bring him inside to Miss Cora, then."

"Do whatever the hell you want. I told you what I think. You done chose sides. That's all there is to it."

Lucas nodded, puffed his cheeks to blow out a long breath, then looked at Lex. "I reckon you might as well come on inside then, Mr. Cranshaw."

Lex moved past Daniel, half expecting the older boy to

try and block his path. But Daniel remained as motionless as he had been. He never even turned to watch as Lex moved toward the door.

There was a rusted screen nailed to a pine frame, and Lucas pulled it open, then stood aside with all the politeness of a schoolboy as he waved Lex on inside.

The cabin was dark, and smelled of spices. It was warmer than he would have expected, and he noticed the windows were all closed. Lucas closed the front door as well, then walked toward a doorway across the long narrow front room. "Come on," he said. "She's out here."

Lex could hear voices now, and he recognized one as belonging to Beatrice Macready. He could only assume the other belonged to her mother. Lucas stopped in the doorway, bending to fit under the low frame, and waited for Lex to catch up.

The back room was part kitchen and part workroom. Lex could see one end of a table and two empty chairs, a wood stove against the rear wall, and a stack of firewood in a coal scuttle, the small logs standing on end beside the stove.

As Lucas moved on through the doorway, Lex could see the back of Beatrice Macready's head and one shoulder. She was leaning forward with her arms stretched out in front of her across the table. Lex stepped all the way in, and saw another, much older, black woman on the opposite side of the table. She held Beatrice's hands in her own upturned palms. She was talking softly as Lex drew close.

Lex stood at one end of the table. The woman looked up at him for a moment, then turned back to her daughter, as if to tell him that family came first. She'd get to him when her priorities permitted.

Beatrice nodded her head slowly as Cora Macready stroked her daughter's hand. "Child," the older woman said, "I wouldn't hurt you for nothing in this world. But the man has to be told. He has to know. Mr. Roy is dead, and he weren't nothing no how, but maybe this man can make it all right again. Like it used to be. They killed Billy, and they got to pay."

Beatrice shook her head violently, but Cora persisted. "Now don't you be telling me no. I'm your mama and I know what's best. You just hush and let me do what I have to do. You know I have to do it. There's no other way."

Beatrice took a deep breath, seemed to hold it forever, then slowly nodded her head, letting the breath out as if it were the last one she'd ever draw. "All right, Mama."

"That's a good child," Cora said. She patted Beatrice on the arm, squeezed both her daughter's hands, then looked at Lex. Staring at the ranger, she spoke to her daughter one more time. "Beatrice, you go on outside with Daniel." Then she looked at Lucas. "You take her outside, boy. I have to talk to this man alone."

Lucas reached a hand out for Beatrice, who turned and looked at the kid for a second, almost as if she weren't sure who he was. He shook his head to reassure her, and Beatrice stood up.

Lex watched her walk to the doorway, where she turned once more, looking past Lucas's shoulder. "Go on, child," Cora said.

When Beatrice was gone, and Lucas had followed

her through the front room and onto the porch, Cora Macready patted the table across from her. Lex took the chair Beatrice had vacated. He looked into the old woman's face. Her skin was like dark copper, as if there were some white blood somewhere in her lineage. Lex knew how that was. You couldn't spend three years in the Confederate army without hearing more than you cared to about such things. She looked so familiar. She reminded him of someone.

The woman seemed to have some inner strength. Her face was perfectly placid, as if there was nothing she hadn't seen or couldn't handle. "What you want to know?" she asked. In contrast to the tender solicitousness of her conversation with her daughter, her voice had now taken on a calm brassiness.

"You sent a letter to Austin, didn't you Mrs. Macready?"

The old woman shook her head.

"I did, yes. Somebody had to."

"I'm not asking you to apologize."

"Nothing to apologize for. The sheriff wasn't going to do nothing. At first, I thought it would just blow over. But when they hung that boy . . . Billy . . . " She stopped, her voice almost cracking, and stared at Lex long and hard. "You got to stop it," she said. "You got to make them pay."

"I need your help."

"No, you don't. I can see that. You don't need nobody's help. What you need is the truth. And that won't be easy to come by. Not here. Not now."

"Why not?"

"These folks is scared. They got a right to be, I guess. But if they won't do nothing to stop it, it'll just keep on gettin' worse. I seen my share of hangin's. And the first one was more than plenty, I don't mind telling you."

Lex nodded to show that he understood, although he found his mind going in circles. He didn't want to push the woman, but he didn't need anyone to tell him what he already knew. He needed someone to tell him what he didn't know. So far, he couldn't tell whether Cora Macready was that person or not.

"You said Billy Otterkill didn't rustle anyone's cattle. Is that right?"

"Yes, that's right. You think I would lie about something like that?"

"No, but . . . "

"He never done it. He was a decent boy. That boy never stole nothing in his life. His daddy would have skinned him alive."

"You seem pretty certain."

"I *am* certain, boy. I don't run my mouth about things I don't know. But I know Billy never done nothing."

"Then why was he hanged?"

"Because *somebody* done something. They wanted to cover it up. They blame Billy, then nobody looks at them."

"Who are 'they,' Mrs. Macready?"

"The ones who done it, of course."

"What about the other hangings?"

"I don't know about them. Not particular. But you find the ones killed Billy, you'll find the ones killed all a them. I know that."

"You know who they are?"

She didn't answer him right away. She leaned back away from the table, her hands braced on its edge to either side. She seemed to be debating something in her own mind. Lex knew she probably didn't trust him. She had no reason to. He was a lawman, and he was a white man. Those was two pretty strong reasons for Cora Macready to be careful what she told him. That she was talking to him at all was remarkable. But something seemed to be pushing her, driving her, her to tell him what she knew, despite her mistrust.

Finally, she shook her head. "Not for sure," she whispered. "But I have my thoughts. I have my reasons for 'em, too."

"I can't put a man in jail without proof, Mrs. Macready."

"You ain't gone put this man in no jail. You gonna have to kill him."

"I'm not a hired gun. Not for the state of Texas or for anybody else."

"Then you the wrong man for the job. They shoulda sent somebody knows how to shoot, not afraid to do it. No matter what. That's what it gonna take."

"You seem sure of that."

"Six men been hanged already, Mister Ranger. Now what you think, the man done that gonna let you take him? That what you think? Then you a bigger fool than you look to be."

Lex smiled.

It took her off guard. "You think that's funny?"

He shook his head. "Yes, I do."

She laughed herself, then. It was deep and genuine. "Then maybe you not as big a fool as I thought."

"I hope not."

"I hope not, too. If you are, you be dead in a week. And I don't know what will happen to Bea . . . to *me.*"

"You liked Billy Otterkill, didn't you?"

"Yes sir, I liked him right enough."

"You mind telling me why?"

"Yes, I do."

"Fair enough. But you're sure he was a scapegoat?"

"A what?"

"You're sure they hanged him to cover something up. To throw suspicion on him for some reason."

"Not for some reason. For one reason. They stealing Mr. Holliman's cows. And when he found them cows all penned up, they had to blame somebody."

"And they just pulled Billy's name out of a hat?"

Cora Macready shook her head. "No. They never done that. They picked him on purpose. They had they reasons."

"What reasons?"

"No sir. You don't need to know that."

"Yes, Mrs. Macready. I do need to know that."

"Naw. You don't."

Lex let it slide for a minute. "Can you tell me who they are?"

"I can, but I'm not gonna. I tell you where to look. You catch them with they hands in the honey. That's all you need do. Isn't it?"

It wasn't really a question, and Lex didn't treat it as

one. "Yes, that's all I need to do."

"Then you stop askin' me questions. You go to that canyon, and you catch'em."

"Mrs. Macready, I . . ."

"Naw. I said all I'm gonna say. I told you what you need. You go to that canyon. That's why you come, isn't it? To get them who hanged Billy and them others?"

"Yes, of course."

"Then you go do it. You don't need to know no more from me. You just find 'em. And the one behind it. You gonna have to shoot him. Shoot him dead. If not, he'll shoot you dead. Dead as a dog. You understand?"

"I think so. But I can't . . ."

"I already told you. I ain't saying no more. Don't need to. Won't."

13

THE sun was setting as Lex eased his mount into the steep slope. The rocky ground was covered with loose scree, and pebbles skipped and rattled away from the roan's hooves. The cascading rocks sounded like hailstones as they clattered down the slope, dislodging others as they rolled and skidded. The horse was being cautious, and Lex let him have his head.

The higher they climbed, the more deliberate the horse's progress became. Off to the west, the soft contours of the New Mexico mountains stretched off into purple blurs at either end of the horizon. He was taking a big chance, and he knew it, but what Mrs. Macready had told him was useless in a court of law. If he was going to make anything stick, if he was going to get a wedge to drive deep into the narrow chink her information provided, he was going to have to work.

He had his head stuck way out, and he could already hear Captain Carmody shouting how lucky he was nobody had chopped it off. And for the moment, that was wishful thinking. He might get it lopped off yet. He could see the light at the end of the tunnel. He just didn't know whether it would burn him to cinders.

The scant vegetation seemed to be changing before his eyes. The clumps of grass that studded the flats were all but gone now. Spikey flowers stabbed out with sudden flashes of bright color. Thorny shrubs, their roots tangled deep into fissures in the slabs of rock under the loose soil, hung here and there on vertical faces, and an occasional scrub oak sprang straight up, ignoring the precipitous angle of the slope.

The sky began to darken a little, and he looked up to see a huge wall of clouds rolling out of the west. Its edges were on fire, and broad bands of light, arranged like feathers in a peacock's tail, sprayed across the sky from behind the thunderhead. Lex crossed his fingers and prayed it wouldn't rain.

He still had a couple of hundred yards to climb, and the sandy soil was slowly giving way to rock. The footing was more secure now, and his mount's hooves cracked sharply every now and then on a stone face swept clean of soil by the wind and the all-too occasional showers.

Lex wanted to be up top before dark. The footing was only part of the reason. He wanted to get a good look at the bottom of the canyon, and he wanted to know every inch of the rim. If Mrs. Macready's information was correct, there'd be no time for anything once the sun came up.

Looking back down at the perilous trail, he was beginning to think he might have made a mistake bringing the big roan. The horse would be of little use to him on the canyon rim. But he couldn't afford to lug everything on his back, and, more than that, he could ill afford to get stranded on foot. Not out here, where, without shade or water, the sun would make soup of his brains in three hours.

The tabletop of the mesa was just ahead of him now, and he had to fight the urge to go even faster. The rim wasn't going anywhere, and if he fell now, he would be a bloody bag of broken bones by the time he stopped rolling. The horse kept shaking its head, trying to free itself of even the slightest tension on the reins, as if it sensed what he was thinking and wanted to make sure Lex didn't do anything foolish.

The sky darkened further, and Lex stared up at the mass of dark clouds. But he could see the western edge now, and knew it wasn't going to rain, at least not here and not now. Already, the darkness had begun to lift a little as the thinner, trailing edge of the clouds, began to slide toward him, letting more sun seep through. As he reached the top, the edge of the clouds' shadow sped toward him like a dark tide on the red rock, and when it finally passed, the sun exploded again and the sky became a clear blue.

Lex dismounted and pulled his horse closer to the rim. He could see down into the canyon, but wasn't close enough to see the floor. He tied the horse to a stunted oak and walked close to the edge. Looking down into the shadowed rocks and scattered small trees, he found himself making short-hand calculations. There wasn't that much cover in the small canyon, but there was enough. He'd have to walk the rim until he found a vantage point that allowed him maximum coverage. He glanced at the sky, and estimated that he had a little over an hour before it was too dark to risk moving close to the rim.

He started off at a brisk walk, staying as close to the edge as he dared, but not without checking each foot before he took a step. The solid-looking rock lay in slabs on the floor and any step might send another huge flake tumbling end over end down to the bottom of the canyon. In some places the walls were nearly two hundred feet high. There was no doubt in his mind that he'd get the chance to make only one misstep. And that it would kill him.

He was halfway around when he found a small cairn. The rocks caught his eye because they looked too neat, as if someone had purposely gathered them, then placed them randomly in an attempt to disguise the fact. Idly, he prodded one of the stones with a toe and it rolled easily to one side. It was sitting flat on the surface and left no depression, a sure sign that it had been recently situated.

Dropping to his knees, he tossed a few more aside, wondering who could have arranged them and why. Now he had a flat rock, roughly the size and shape of the top of a night-table. The last rock was heavy and it slipped from his grip the first time he tried to lift it. Digging his fingers more deeply into the dirt along opposing edges, he got a secure grip and pulled. The rock came up easily. He found himself staring at a small, flat package, wrapped in oil cloth.

Lex lifted the package, his fingers already groping through the cloth, trying to guess what it concealed. It felt flat and hard, but wasn't wood or metal. He unfolded the ends of the oil cloth and peeled away one layer, then a second of the same material.

It was a school tablet.

He started to open it, then sat back on his haunches. Letting his mind have free rein, he tried to prepare himself for what he might find, knowing that it was unlikely that it had anything to do with the problem confronting him, and knowing too that its placement almost certainly connected it to the rustling.

He opened the faded reddish paper cover. In a neat, childlike hand, he saw the scrawl—William James Otterkill, 1864. He started flipping the pages, pausing just long enough to notice the penmanship. So far, it was nothing but school exercises. The spelling drills of a punctilious teacher. The shaky hand of a child fumbling his way through the elements of arithmetic. And history notes, neither detailed nor carefully done, as if Billy Otterkill didn't give much of a damn about what happened before he had been born. But then, Lex thought, so few of us do.

Flipping the pages more rapidly, he found a few blanks, then some numbers. They were more legible than those in the math exercises, as if written by someone else . . .

or by an older Billy Otterkill. The numbers didn't make much sense, by themselves. Turning another page, he found the same numbers, this time each entered next to a date. Two columns marched down the page:

March 11 — 29
March 23 — 1
April 17 — 42
May 3 — 27

There were more entries, and Lex flipped back to the first page of figures. It looked now as if whoever had written them was working on a running total. But what was being counted? Lex glanced at the sky again, then shook his head and rewrapped the notebook and stuck in inside his shirt.

It was getting dark, and he still had a lot of ground to cover. The numbers could wait. As he worked his way toward the back of the canyon, then started around to the other side, he found it harder to see clearly into the bottom of the canyon. It was full of shadows now, and they hid more and more details of the canyon floor.

By the time he was halfway along the far wall, he couldn't see anything except the largest rocks and the tallest trees. Everything else was hidden under a dark blur. The sun was behind him, and he could see its fading red light dying his skin bright scarlet.

Reluctantly, Lex started back toward his horse, picking his way carefully, like a blind man in a maze. He drifted away from the rim now, knowing he couldn't see the fissures in the rock and that a trip might send him hurtling over the rim and down onto the rocks.

He could move more quickly across the back wall, which was the front edge of a flat mesa. There were rocks and mesquite bushes, but nothing he couldn't deal with at a fast walk. The moon would be up in a couple of hours, and he thought about waiting for its light, but was too anxious. He wanted to sit and think, to try and understand what he had just found. He could feel the flat package inside his shirt, pressing against his chest like an insistent hand.

The more he thought about the columns, the more he believed the information was worthless. Unless he knew what the numbers referred to, they would tell him nothing, and tell a court less. And the less likely it seemed he would ever get to the bottom of the strange and tangled puzzle.

An hour later, he was getting close to his mount. He could hear the horse somewhere up ahead, but still couldn't pick it out among the rocks and clumps of brush. He slowed a little to catch his breath, walking now like a man who had no place to go, and all the time in the world to get there.

He had a long night ahead of him. There wasn't a thing he could do until sunrise, and even then, it wasn't likely he could get any closer to the truth. When he finally reached his horse, he undid his bedroll and scraped a flat space free of stones. He knelt, spread the bedroll on the hard ground, took off his gunbelt and lay down to stare at the sky.

He found his mind drifting in circles. At their center
was a woman. He couldn't see her clearly, but he knew
she was an old black woman. Cora Macready? He didn't
think so. But someone very like her. And then he knew.
And he was back there, lying in the mud, the guns of
Shiloh a steady thunder in his ears. He could feel the
bullet again as it tore through his shoulder, the searing
pain as he tried to move. And couldn't.

Then he could see her more clearly. He'd woken up,
the sun beating down on him. The mud of two days'
rain plastered on him like cement. And she'd looked at
him without speaking, the sun behind her, her sad face
shielding him from its relentless glare, a circle of almost
white light surrounding her as she bent over him. Then
she'd gone away. He'd closed his eyes, wondering if
he'd been dreaming. When he opened them again, it
was because someone had moved his arm and the pain
had made him scream. He could still see the sun, but it
had moved an hour, maybe two.

She'd brought her son and together they had brought
him to a ramshackle cabin in the Tennessee hills. The
woman had refused to talk to him, not even to tell him
her name. But he'd found out. He'd kept at the boy until
he wore him down. So like Cora Macready, she was.
Strong, stronger than any woman he'd known before.
Not physical strength but strength of something deeper,
more elusive. A soul, the preacher would have called it,
but it wasn't that either. It was a strength that came from
someplace deep inside her, and she didn't even seem to
know just how brave a thing it was she had done. Saving

a man who had been fighting to keep her a slave, for no reason other than that he was hurt and needed help. She gave it.

And he'd never had a chance to thank her. She'd been killed a week later, a stray minié ball, her son said, from some Yankee trooper's musket.

Miss Emily. That was as much of her name as he ever knew. He still thought of her often. He wouldn't be here to think at all if it hadn't been for her. And there was something about Cora Macready that was just like Miss Emily.

When the moon came up, he was still awake. He'd forgotten about the discomfort as he watched the sky fill with silver light, turning everything around him pale gray. The gnarled mesquite looked as if it had been carved out of coal, but everything else seemed made of pewter. Even the stones seemed to glow the least little bit. He was awake in the middle of a dream, he thought. That was the only place he had seen things like this. Or was it a nightmare?

Far out across the flats, he could hear the yip of coyotes. Their sudden howls sounded as if they were right behind him, and when his nerves settled down again, he would try to locate them more precisely. He wasn't going to sleep. He knew that now.

Lex got up and shifted the bedroll a few feet until he could lean back against a large rock. Taking the book out of his shirt, he tilted it toward the moon and flipped through the pages. It was hard to see the writing, but if he leaned close, he could manage.

One more time, he followed page after page of school-work, then got to the blank pages. This time he noticed something he hadn't seen before. A couple of pages had been torn out of the book. Feeling the shredded ends with his fingertips he tried to count them. Three, maybe four, he thought. No more than that.

What was on the missing pages?

On a hunch, he lit a match and held it close to the first blank page. There was something there, depressions in the paper, but the light wasn't good enough to read the shallow impressions. Maybe at sunup.

He sighed and pushed on through the numbers, then all the way to the back of the book. Dozens of empty pages. Even the inside back cover was blank. He'd have to figure it out from here, working with the numbers alone, or find the missing pages.

By the time the moon started to set, he was no closer to a solution. He closed the book, rewrapped it one more time and tucked it back inside his shirt. The sky was getting gray and it would be less than an hour before the sun came up. He felt like he was on the last leg of a fool's errand, but it was too late to do anything but follow it all the way through.

Then the sky caught fire and another day began.

14

EX sat close to the rim. He held the binoculars in his lap and looked out across the flat, arid expanse. Carney was fifteen miles away, not even a curl of smoke on the horizon to betray its existence. He was waiting, not quite sure what for, but he knew why.

So far the flats were empty. Maybe it was time to look at the notebook again, he thought, Pulling the flat package from his shirt, he thumbed through the pages until he found the place where the leaves were missing. He could see the squiggly lines he'd noticed the night before. They were still hard to read, but he was convinced they were handwriting. The stubby pencil Billy Otterkill had used had required pressure. The pressure had gone right on through and indented the pages below.

Tilting the flat page until he found the best angle, he

tried to decipher the scrawl. There were overlapping lines
as writing from one page crushed the next. The latest was
the deepest, but none of it was all that legible. He could
make out something that could have been "Billy," as if
it had been a signature on a short letter, but Lex just
couldn't be sure.

Near the top, there was a clear impression, but it wasn't
as deep as the others. A salutation?

Shifting the page to try and fill the scrawl with shadow, he could make out a few letters, but it was still a
puzzle. There was an *e* and a space, *la* and something
that could have been a *t* or an *f* or maybe an *h*, he just
didn't know.

Disappointed, he stuffed the notebook back into his
shirt and looked down into the canyon.

Cora Mcready had told him the answer was in this canyon, and he was determined to sit here until hell, or at
least East Texas, froze over, if he had to. The sun was
already blindingly white by eight o'clock. The flatlands
looked as if all color was being bleached out as he waited.
There was no green left, leached away by the sun and
leaving behind only dull gray. The soil was so fine and
so dry, it reflected a blinding glare that hurt his eyes. The
rocks lost all definition. They had turned to lumps of pale
color against the otherwise uniform glare.

Despite the passing of the thunderhead the night before, there wasn't a single cloud in the sky. Even its
color had dwindled down to a faint blue stain against
the yellow-white air. His horse was restless, but Lex was
determined to spend all day if necessary, and the next

day, too, if it should be required.

Every fifteen minutes since the sun had come up, he'd swept the glasses across the half circle spread out below him. So far, he hadn't seen a single sign of life. Not a bird in the sky, or a rat on the ground had broken the stillness. The longer he sat, the hotter the ground became and he thought he could hear it humming with the intense heat, the way a griddle will vibrate then sputter when it's finally hot enough to boil a drop of water away into nothing.

He had his Winchester cradled across his knees, not knowing if he would need it, but not knowing either if he would have time to get it if he did need it. He was ready for anything, as ready as he could be, knowing nothing and expecting anything.

By nine, his resolve was starting to weaken, as if the unyielding heat had softened it the way it would a candle left all day in the open. But this was his best chance. He reached into his shirt again. Beside him on the rock, he set down the notebook of Billy Otterkill. It was still a mystery, but he couldn't shake the feeling that it was the key to everything, the map that would help him put it all together. Maybe having it in the open would help.

At ten, he saw a small cloud far out across the open flats. He panned forward with the glasses, starting in the canyon mouth and slowly marching the glasses out into the open plains. The stray clumps of grass looked stiff as wires, their motionless blades covered with fine dust. He found the cloud, but could make nothing of it. Even through the binoculars, it was too small, too shapeless to tell him much. Something, or someone, was moving

across the near desert, but so slowly he couldn't be sure
in what direction.

By ten-thirty, he knew the cloud was coming his way,
and by ten-forty-five, he could see a mule team drawing an old wagon. There was a man in the driver's seat
and two men on horseback beside the rickety wooden
schooner. In the glare, their faces were just blurs under
tilted hat brims.

He watched them off and on for the next hour. As they
grew larger, it was apparent they were heading in the general direction of the canyon just beneath his feet, but he
had no way of telling whether it was their goal or merely
an accident of their passage. He could see the men more
clearly now, clearly enough to be certain he knew none
of them.

The wagon-bed was covered with a canvas roof on
metal hoops, and he could see nothing of what it might
be carrying. As the sun reached a point directly overhead,
the wagon turned slightly and headed directly toward the
canyon mouth. Lex backed away from the rim rock and
lay behind a boulder, propping the glasses on the stone
where he could reach them in a hurry. He could see the
team and wagon with the naked eye, if he squinted, and
closed his eyes to rest them a little, tilting his hat forward
and leaning his forehead on his folded arms.

He hated waiting more than anything in the world. But
this was one time when there was nothing he could do
about it. There was no law against driving a wagon across
the floor of hell if that's what you wanted to do. The men
far below him might be crazy, but that wasn't a crime,

either. So he waited some more.

He could hear the creaking of the weathered boards and the greaseless hubs of the ancient wheels. Less than a mile from the mouth of the canyon, the wagon and its two-man escort were still the only moving things. Lex watched the last agonizing mile until the wagon pulled through the mouth of the box canyon. Creeping close to the edge, he started down on the wagon's canvas cover as it rocked toward the rear wall, turned in a half circle, then squealed to a halt.

The two horsemen dismounted and waited for the driver to climb down out of the wagon. Through the glasses, Lex watched them light cigarettes, talking among themselves for a few moments, then break open a bottle of whiskey. He was beginning to wonder if maybe all he'd stumbled on was a way-station for a trader of some kind, maybe with some whiskey for the Indians, maybe nothing so exotic.

The men passed the bottle back and forth, each one wiping his mouth on his sleeve before taking a swig, then handing it on. When they were done drinking, one of the horsemen remounted and rode slowly back toward the mouth of the canyon. Lex watched him dismount again, tie his horse in a clump of small willows, then start to climb up a steep wing of rock and loose dirt until he found a place he could sit.

The horseman had a rifle with him, and leaned it against the rock behind him. He looked out across the flatlands, apparently expecting someone. He wore binoculars around his neck, but didn't bother to use them.

Lex examined him closely through his own field glasses, but after a couple of minutes, he was certain he'd never seen the man before.

So, maybe Cora Macready was right after all. He'd wait and see.

Turning his attention to the wagon, Lex watched as the driver gathered dry mesquite and heaped it in a small mound to start a fire. When the small branches caught, he went to the back of the wagon and opened the canvas cover. He pulled something out which Lex didn't recognize at first, because it was so unexpected. But there was no doubt about it. The man had taken a small log out of the wagon bed. He then withdrew an ax and a wedge and proceeded to split the log into chunks of firewood, stacked them within reach of the small fire, then pulled two more logs out of the wagon. He said something to the other horseman, now sitting on the ground with his back against the canyon wall. The horseman waved a hand, spat in the general direction of the driver, then slid down the wall and covered his eyes with his hat.

Lex turned the glasses on the flats again. Another cloud, this one larger and less compact, was rolling in now. It was dust kicked up on a broad front, but it was still too distant for him to tell for sure what was causing it. At first glance it looked like it might be a large band of mounted men, but as he twiddled the focus knob, he brought the dark leading edge of the cloud into sharper focus. It wasn't horsemen after all. It was cattle, sixty or seventy head, moving toward the canyon.

It started to make sense now. The firewood, the fire, the

wagon. It was a work team, getting ready for branding. But why here? There was only one answer that made sense. And now he started to think of those numbers in the notebook. Head of cattle? Rustled steers by the twenties and thirties, cut out of herds or strays rounded up and penned someplace until they could be moved to the canyon for brand doctoring?

Lex felt his gut clench. The answer was getting closer, rolling toward him ahead of a cloud of dust. He watched the cattle for several minutes, trying to pick out the riders, but they were all in the drag or on the wing, obscured by the thick cloud. He'd have to wait until the small herd was brought in and the dust settled.

He watched for another hour. It was well after midday, and the sun was still hammering down on him. He backed away from the edge of the canyon and took a sip of water. It was warm enough to do the wash, and it tasted of bitter salt and metal, but at least it was wet.

By three o'clock, the first cattle reached the mouth of the canyon and he could hear the pounding of their hooves as well as the shrill whistles of the drovers, who were funneling the animals through the narrow mouth with flailing arms and shouts. The animals continued on to the rear of the canyon where they huddled against the steep rock face of the back wall, their bellows gradually dying down as they settled in.

There were four drovers, and Lex scrutinized each one, trying at least to etch his features in his mind if he couldn't identify him. One of them, a big man who appeared to be three or four inches over six feet, looked vaguely familiar, but the glare and the shadow of his hat made it difficult to be sure.

Lex backed away from the rim and got to his feet. Staying far enough away from the edge so that he couldn't be seen, he sprinted along the north wall of the canyon. He wanted to get close, above the wagon if he could, to see exactly what the men were planning. With every minute, it looked less and less possible that there could be an innocent explanation, but he had to be sure.

It took fifteen minutes to reach the corner and he stopped and lay on his belly to crawl close again. At the mouth of the canyon, the lookout was still on his perch, the glasses around his neck and his Winchester in his hands now. Creeping close to the edge, he looked down into the milling herd of cattle. The wagon was fifty or sixty yards farther on.

Some of the firewood had been stacked on the small blaze, and as Lex watched, the driver went to the back of his wagon and poked his head through an opening in the canvas. Lex heard the clink of metal on metal, the driver backed away from the wagon and turned with three branding irons in his hand.

Lex couldn't see the business end of the irons plainly, and couldn't risk the glasses. He watched the driver squat by the fire, poke the irons one by one into the blaze, kicking up a column of sparks. One of the drovers walked back to his horse and climbed into the saddle. He was joined by the second of the wagon's guardians.

The two men moved toward the cattle, now standing around in the corner, and got a rope on one of the smaller cows. They worked the cow away from the herd, then led it toward the wagon. Getting the ropes tight, and cutting down on the lead, the two riders maneuvered the steer into a small clearing a few yards from the fire, then one of them dismounted and dogged the animal to its side, looped a rope around its front and hind legs, then stood up and clapped his hands.

He said something Lex couldn't hear, but it made the other man laugh. He walked to the fire and stood looking down at the irons, reached out and took one by the heavy iron loop on its free end and pulled it out of the flames. He looked over at the other horseman, then shoved the iron back into the fire and walked toward the wagon driver, who said something, turned away, then turned back. The cowboy nodded and walked back to the fire.

Lex had to see exactly what was happening. He needed to know what brand the cattle bore, and what brand was being burned in on top of it. But it was too risky to get closer now. He needed a break and he needed it soon.

15

LEX watched three of the hands ride back out of the canyon. It trimmed the odds, but they were still uncomfortable. He gave the tall man one more look, but still couldn't see him clearly enough to place. He was certain he'd seen him before, though. There was something about the swagger, the slope of the man's shoulders. He worried over it for a few minutes, but it kept sliding away from, like a word on the tip of the tongue. If he could leave it alone, it would 'come to him.

There was no easy way down into the canyon. Lex knew it was going to have to be on foot, and in from the front. But first he had to get down. Without being seen. He jammed his Winchester back into its boot and rooted in his saddlebags for a box of shells, which he dumped into his shirt pockets. He didn't like leaving the horse, and he was especially not happy about being so far away from the roan once things got hot. Grabbing the Winchester again, he took one more look. He was as ready as he was ever going to be.

It was a long shot, but there was no other way. The four men now left below were his best chance, and he couldn't pass it up. Backing away from the roan, he broke for the back end of the canyon, sprinting flat out and slowing only when he reached the first turn. He had to stay back away from the canyon rim, because the sentry was still sitting on his perch.

Lex was going to have to work his way down the southern lip without tipping off the picket. One loose stone was all it would take, and as he started the descent, he crossed his fingers. The first fifty feet was not too bad. The mesa sloped gradually, and the footing was mostly solid rock. All he had to worry about here was the sound of his boots on the stone.

He cleared the first leg, and things started to get more dicey. The slope was still gradual, in fact much more gentle than the side he'd come up, but the dirt was loose and studded with rocks the size of his fist. There was no way one could fall without sending up a clatter that would wake the dead . . . and probably create a couple more.

He had to place his feet cautiously, digging his heels in through the soft dirt, trying to bite into the rock below it. Some of the loose soil sifted away with every step, hissing as it slid down the slope. He kicked a rock, and it slid a couple of feet, rolled ten more, then disappeared against a mesquite bush. Lex held his breath, waiting for the rock to rush on through the low hanging branches and bounce on down. But his luck was holding. The stone bounced into a low limb and hung suspended there as the branch rose and fell under the impact.

Lex got on hands and knees. Half sliding and half crawling, he got close enough to the mesquite to reach the rock. Straining to keep from sliding into the thorns, he stretched his hand as far as he could, felt his fingertips brush the rock and saw the branch sway slightly. He allowed himself to slide a couple of inches more, finally closing the rock in his fist just as it started to fall off the branch.

With a sigh of relief, he hefted the rock, then put it down and leaned on it to imbed it in the loose soil. There was more cover now, and Lex started to zigzag from rock to bush to boulder to shrub. It was taking more time than he wanted to spend, but the alternative was a headlong rush that would give the sentry enough time to grab some cover. If he got off a shot, the surprise was gone and it was a useless assault, and probably suicide, one man against four. In this terrain, unless the one man were an Apache, there could only be one outcome.

The next leg of the descent was the trickiest. He'd have to be in the open for nearly seventy feet, and he could barely make out the brim of the sentry's hat. One noise would alert the guard, and Lex would be a sitting duck. The slope was too steep for him to move quickly, and he would have no chance at all to get out of the way of the first slug sent in his direction.

Moving right until even the hat brim disappeared, Lex

lay on his stomach. He didn't like being so vulnerable, but the more of his body he could keep in contact with the steep slope, the more control he'd have over his descent. He started to crawl, pulling himself along with his elbows. Every couple of feet he had to stop and reach out to pull the loose stones out of the way, as much for comfort as for silence. He was starting to feel like a lizard as the sun slammed down on his back and his chest and stomach felt the heat of the soil even through his clothing.

Lex was aiming for a clump of scrub oak that seemed securely perched on the edge of a steep drop. If he lost control, the oak would arrest his slide, and it was also the only cover for twenty yards in any direction. Far behind him, he could hear the bellowing of the steers as the other three men continued their leisurely branding.

In the back of his mind, Lex was toying with the next step, wondering how long the men intended to stay. If they had already made arrangements for the cattle, they might run them out as soon as the branding was finished. If he was right that the numbers in Billy's notebook represented head of cattle overbranded on different occasions, the small herd below was by far the largest so far. It might mean they were planning to pen them here awhile, then drive them to some market, possibly in Mexico, where they'd go for ten cents on the dollar. But ten percent of something extra was always better than nothing. If they ran them north, they'd do even better. Buyers in Kansas were none too particular where beeves came from, as long as they could walk and had a little meat on their bones.

Lex lost control of his momentum as he neared the oak, and he started picking up speed. A cascade of sand swirled ahead of him and he could hear it hissing as it rushed over the edge. Reaching out with his left hand, he was able to slow himself, plowing a ridge of loose soil with the heel of this hand, but his momentum brought him around in a half circle and he felt his legs swinging out over the edge of the drop.

In desperation, he threw the Winchester back behind him and grabbed onto the base of the oak with both hands. He swung down and slammed into the rock wall as the Winchester skidded toward him. Letting go with one hand, he reached out to snag the rifle and brought it up and behind the oak, then grabbed onto the tangled roots. The impact with the wall had knocked the breath from his lungs and he gasped for air as his shoulder sockets slowly caught on fire.

He knew he could hang there just so long before his muscles cramped. Glancing back over his shoulder, he found himself looking at a sheer drop of nearly fifty feet. There was no way he could survive it uninjured, if at all. Taking a deep breath, he started to haul himself back up, raising himself high enough to snake both arms around the trunk of the small oak.

Swinging his left leg up, he tried to get it over the edge, but missed on the first try. When his body swung back down, his shoulders groaned, and he winced with the pain. Trying again, he managed to hook his foot on the edge, then wiggled it back up the slippery slope a few inches.

He heard the roots of the oak begin to creak as his weight slowly stretched them. Sand was beginning to pour from the base of the tree, and he knew it was only a matter of time before the small tree gave way altogether. He tried to raise his body enough to slide his leg a little farther uphill, then used his arms to lever himself up enough to get his belt buckle and one shoulder over the edge. This relieved the stress on the oak and on his aching joints.

Lex lay there panting, sweat trickling into his eyes and running down his back in a sticky stream. Slowly, he started to roll over, trying to get himself farther uphill and away from the edge. Moving cautiously, he managed to get most of his weight back on the ledge. Pulling against the oak, he dragged himself forward a couple of feet until he could lie behind the small tree.

In the back of his mind was the fear that he had been heard, but there was nothing he could do about it now. Rolling onto his back, he grabbed the Winchester, then swung his body around to dig in his heels and push himself back up the hill a little. If he were careful, he should be able to creep across the slope until he could find a way to get down. Closer to the mouth of the canyon, a wing of red rock, almost like a flying buttress, jutted out and dropped to the floor just beside the mouth.

Layer after layer of rock, weathered and broken by heat and cold, offered him dozens of handholds. If he could just reach it without sliding off the edge. Pressing himself flat against the burning heat of the sand, he crept inch by inch, his legs splayed and arms stretched like wings to keep him from rolling or sliding.

When he reached a flat shelf of rock, he crawled onto it and lay with his arms cradling his head, sucking in air and letting his heart settle into a normal rhythm. He used the time to listen. The bellow of the cattle still drifted upward, and there was no other noise that might indicate he'd been discovered.

Examining the buttresslike flare of stratified rock, he decided he could risk the climb. He knew the going would be precarious, because far below he could see mounds of broken stone that had crumbled from the flaking edges of the rock. But there was no other way down. He hadn't bothered to bring a rope because there was nothing he could secure it to. It was hands and feet, climbing down the rock wall like a beetle or a lizard.

The rock flared away from a shelf which jutted out over the floor of the valley. He crawled out on it, jammed the Winchester down his back and through his belt, and swung his legs out and down. Lex hugged the wall, ignoring the prod of broken edges of sharp stone, and felt with his feet for a small ledge that would take his weight. This was going to be the worst part of the climb, because once he started, he was committed to it. If anything gave way, he'd fall all the way.

Lex felt a sense of urgency now and had to fight against the impulse to scramble recklessly. Foot by foot, he clambered down. Ten feet later, it looked as if he still had as far to go. After twenty feet, he was finding his rhythm, moving easily, finding each little ledge with his feet, shifting his hands confidently and inching down another step, then another.

One small shelf broke off under his foot, and he hung on, his cheek pressed against the stone while pieces of rock showered down the last thirty feet. If he was going to be heard, that was the time. When nothing happened, he let his breath out slowly and started down again. This time he tried to hold himself in check, but the closer he got to the ground, the faster he climbed, as if time were running out on him, or as if the earth were drawing him against his will.

When his feet finally touched bottom, he clung to the rock for a long moment, listening to the rasp of his breath in his throat. Slowly, he backed away from the jagged stone. He looked up, still not convinced he'd made it. Sixty feet, straight down. Now, all he had to do was find the sentry.

As near as he could tell, Lex was still fifteen or twenty feet above the guard. He moved to his right, climbed around a rounded boulder, then scrambled up on top of it. He could see the hat brim now, more clearly, and he could see the sun-reddened skin of the cowhand where it disappeared into a collar that hadn't seen the hands of a laundress in a long while.

It would be an easy shot. But he hadn't risked breaking his neck to do what he could have done from above. It had to be quick, but above all, it had to be quiet. He had to take the sentry down without alerting the other three men. Creeping across the top of the rock, he risked a glance back into the canyon. He could still hear the cattle, more sedate now, and the smoke from the branding fire had died down a bit, as if it were being allowed to burn itself out.

Looking at the guard again, Lex saw that he had two choices. One, going straight down over the rock and up a steep face of dirt and loose rock, was the most direct. But it was also the less desirable. The other would take longer, but it would let him get above the sentry and drop straight in behind him. It was the only reasonable way to go.

Lex backed off the boulder and dropped to the ground. He bent to pull off his boots, then started forward again, leaving the Winchester strapped behind him and loosening the Bowie knife in its sheath. He had a ledge to negotiate, but first he had to get to it. That meant going back up the same sort of jagged face he'd come down, but only eight or nine feet, until he could get to the shelf and inch across.

On his bootless feet, the stone felt hard and hot. But he gritted his teeth and dug his toes into the narrow crevices and hauled himself to the shelf. Once up top, it was a short sprint and a jump, twelve, maybe fifteen feet to the ground, right behind the sentry. From his angle, he could tell that the sentry couldn't be seen by the men in the back of the canyon. If he got to the guard before a shot was fired, he'd be home free.

Lex balanced on the balls of his feet, then broke into a sprint. He launched himself feet first, bending his legs and planting his knees squarely in the sentry's back. The full weight of his body slammed the guard to the ground. The sentry's rifle flew from his grasp and dropped a dozen feet before landing on its butt and teetering a moment.

The sentry was stunned by the impact and rolled to one side, struggling to get out from under Lex's weight. Automatically, even unthinkingly, he reached for his pistol. Lex moved quickly as the gun cleared the holster. He brought the knife down hard, blade first, on the cowhand's chest. The sharp crack of the blade on rib-bone sounded like stone on stone, and the guard rolled over and lay still.

Lex chewed his lower lip for a moment, looking back toward the end of the canyon. Now, all he had to do was take out the remaining three men.

16

LEX left the sentry where he fell, and went back to get his boots. The canyon was nearly half a mile deep, and he had to get to the other three men before they took it into their heads to leave. He regretted having to kill the guard, but the man had left him no alternative. And he needed at least one of the men alive. Someone had to hand him the next link in the chain. Cora Macready had made it plain that she had given him all the help she was going to give. He was on his own now. She had pointed him in the right direction and given him a push. But the momentum wouldn't last long.

He could still hear the cattle milling around, an occasional bellow, probably as a rope was looped over the neck of another steer for branding. There couldn't be too many left, and once the work was done, the hands were almost certain to cut and run. They couldn't afford to get caught with the cattle. The only question was whether they would drive the beeves themselves or leave them for someone else to pick up.

Picking his way through the rocks along the right-hand wall of the canyon, Lex pushed himself to make up ground. He knew a clock was ticking, but he didn't know just how much time he had left. That it wasn't much was certain.

The sun was already well past its zenith, and the shadow of the rear wall of the canyon was beginning to stretch slowly across the floor. The curling smoke from the branding fire continued to thin out, and Lex guessed he had no more than a half-hour before the last steer would be overbranded. Once that happened, he might find himself on foot trying to run down three men on horseback or in a wagon. If he went back now to get his mount, he'd never get back in time.

He could hear the men shouting to one another, but he wasn't close enough to understand what was being said. As he closed on the back wall, the voices grew louder, and he was able to pick out an occasional word, although nothing that made any sense.

He caught his first glimpse a moment later. It wasn't much, just the brim of a hat. The man was on horseback and he flashed past a notch between two boulders. Lex saw the rope, saw it rise, then disappear as the horseman tossed it. A second later, a steer gave a bellow of protest. Lex could hear the cowhand grunting as he worked the steer.

Slipping into the notch, he found himself staring

squarely into the eyes of one of the cowhands, who stood on the far side of the fire. The hand's face seemed to freeze for a second, then he shouted, his arm stabbing toward Lex as he went for his gun.

Lex ducked down behind the nearest rock as the first crack of gunfire echoed off the canyon walls. The first shot must have gone high, because it hit nothing, but the second slammed into the rocks and whined off into the distance.

Lex dropped to his belly and wormed his way over a layer of broken stone, trying to find better cover. He was only a few yards from the right-hand wall, and squirmed into a crevice with his back against it. The shouting stopped almost immediately. Two more shots cracked, and the bullets glanced off the rocks he'd left behind.

He brought his Winchester around and tried to squeeze between the boulder and the wall to get a line on one of the men. It grew very quiet now as the men stopped shouting. He could hear heavy steps on the sand and broken rock as one of the men, somewhere off to the left, charged toward him. For a second, Lex could see a flash of light blue cloth, probably a shirt, but it was gone before he could draw a bead.

He had come so close. Now he had to worry about staying alive. If he could have taken the men without killing them, he would have had the bird he needed right in his hand. But these men were not going to go down without a fight. Taking them alive had to take a backseat to keeping his own hide intact.

He shinnied up along the wall, wedging himself in behind the rounded face of the rock. He was three feet off the ground, but he still couldn't see anything. Leaning out to the right, he could see the wagon, but there was no one near it. The plume of smoke from the branding fire continued to drift up toward the sky, blurring until it was all but invisible by the time it got up around the rim rock.

Lex squeezed all the way through and nearly lost his grip on the rifle as he slipped to the ground on the far side of the rock. He stumbled, caught his balance with one hand on the wall, sprinted over a loose pile of broken rock. The stones clacked against one another and his feet kept slipping out from under him as he tried to get to the next cover.

He stumbled again and went down hard on his knees. The Winchester skidded away and as he reached for it, he heard a voice not ten feet away.

"He's over here somewhere," it shouted.

Lex got his hand on the butt of the Winchester and was hauling it back toward his body as a cowhand turned the corner. The man saw him just as Lex got his finger through the trigger guard. He rolled to his right, pulling the Winchester toward him, then pressing it flat as he rolled over it. He heard the crack, and chips of rock dug into his shoulder as the bullet narrowly missed him.

He brought the rifle around, found the gunman under his sight. The man was already thumbing back the hammer, when Lex said, "Just hold it. Put that gun down."

The man grinned and brought his Colt up from his hip.

He was reaching out toward Lex with the pistol. His lips curled back over his teeth and Lex squeezed the trigger. It seemed to happen slowly as the man pulled his gun back. It went off, but the shot went wide.

It looked as if the man were trying to back away from the impact of the heavy Winchester slug. His body seemed to curl around the bullet. His pistol clattered on the ground and his feet slowly went out from under him as he stumbled back. One hand went to his gut, and Lex could already see the bright trickle of blood between his fingers. The other hand went toward Lex, palm up, the fingers spread wide, as if to ward off another shot.

He fell heavily.

Lex scrambled to his feet and raced toward the gunman. He kicked the Colt away as one hand clawed its way across the stones trying to reach the gun. Almost as an afterthought, Lex noticed that one of the grips had come loose and lay on the stone in two pieces.

"Ray, you all right?"

The voice came from somewhere out beyond the rocks. Lex looked toward the gunman, who still pressed one hand against his bleeding gut. His mouth moved, but no sound came out, then his jaw went slack as a bubble of blood expanded then burst, sending a trickle of drool down over the chin and onto the man's neck. Lex saw the blood seep toward the collar. He was almost frozen. The voice called again.

"Hey, Ray, where the hell you at?"

The shout galvanized Lex, and he bent to retrieve the man's Colt, tucking it into his belt. He tiptoed closer to the huge slab of red stone that lay off to the left. Somewhere beyond it, and by the sound of the voice, not that far, the second hand was closing in.

Lex dropped to one knee and held the Winchester ready. The second hand called again, his voice more tentative now. "Ray? You all right? Ray, damn it, what's going on?"

The footsteps on the broken rock suddenly stopped. The man was holding his ground, waiting for Roy to answer him. Smart, Lex thought. Real smart. He got to his feet and moved forward, keeping in a low crouch until he was flush up against the back of the next big boulder.

"That you, Ray?" The question sounded farther away, as if the man had backed up, trying to put a little distance between himself and the uncertainty.

Then heavy footsteps. Lex braced for a charge, but the steps were moving the other way. He peered around the rock in time to catch a glimpse of the hand dodging through a cluster of rocks, zigzagging among the stones and looking over his shoulder. He spotted Lex and stopped in his tracks.

Whirling, he aimed his Colt and fired twice. Lex ducked down and when he peered out again, the man was gone. He could still hear footsteps, then a voice as the retreating hand shouted, "Davey, something's wrong. Ray don't answer. I think he's been hit."

A more distant voice shouted back, "How many?"

"Seen only one. There may be more, though. I dunno for sure."

The next sound he heard sent a chill through him. Hooves, coming toward him. He heard one horse, maybe two. The sound stopped for a moment, then a nicker and the hooves started again, this time clearly two mounts. Lex dodged through the rocks, putting some ground between himself and the last place they could have seen him.

Turning a corner, he saw two mounted men, fifty yards apart, one moving toward the mouth of the canyon to cut off his retreat. The other was moving more cautiously, bobbing among the boulders, his eyes sweeping the rocks for the slightest trace of the invader.

Lex found some cover and waited for the searcher to break into the clear. He followed the man closely, keeping the Winchester cocked and aimed. He felt like he could see the man even through the rocks. It was as if there was some invisible connection between them as he tracked. The horseman appeared for a second, and Lex squeezed off a shot, but the bullet went high, narrowly missing the man as he leaned to the left for something.

He dropped off his mount now and Lex could hear him moving through the stones. Lex cut to his right, moving parallel to the wall, trying to outflank the man. He saw him in profile for a second, brought up the rifle, but the man was gone again before he could aim.

Lex climbed over the rocks, looking for a height advantage. It would expose him to the other man, but at long range, it was a risk he could afford. On top of a flat rock, Lex could see the man's horse, now empty, but there was no trace of the cowhand.

Lex held his breath, waiting for that one break. Grabbing a loose piece of rock, he lobbed it in among the boulders, hoping to draw a shot, but the man didn't react. Patience, he kept telling himself, you have to have patience.

Again, he heard footsteps on the loose stones, this time off to his left. He looked toward the sound in time to see the cowhand stepping out from behind a boulder. His Winchester was already trained on Lex, and his lips were twisted in a strange grin, as if he'd just thought of a joke.

Lex rolled to his right, losing his balance and falling off the rock as the cowhand's gun went off. Twisting in the air, Lex broke his fall with his feet, but fell flat on his back as they went out from under him. He lost his grip on his rifle. He heard the Winchester's lever as the man rushed toward him, and Lex rolled to his left, getting flat against the rock and drawing his Colt.

The man charged around the rock, saw Lex and pulled the trigger just as Lex squeezed off a round from his Colt. Something tore through the flesh of his left arm. The man stopped in his tracks, his cheeks puffing out as the bullet slammed into his chest and drove the air from his lungs. He staggered backward two steps, clawed at the Winchester's lever and managed only to get it open before losing his grip and sitting down hard. He leaned awkwardly against the stone, staring at Lex but no longer trying to move.

His jaw went slack and his tongue lolled out of his mouth as his head tilted to one side, pushing his hat up and half off. Lex clapped a hand over his bleeding biceps, and got slowly to his feet.

The ranger knelt beside the cowhand and reached for his throat. There was no pulse, and Lex closed each of the staring eyes with a thumb. He looked toward the mouth of the canyon. The remaining hand was charging toward him now, still on horseback, his rifle extended like an accusing finger. He fired once, jerked another shell home and fired a second time as Lex pulled the trigger on his Colt.

The rider jerked oddly, then Lex saw the smear of blood high on his shoulder as the horseman wheeled his mount and headed back toward the mouth of the canyon.

Lex fired again but the horseman was already out of pistol range. He thought about his own horse, but knew he'd lose too much time going after it and ran toward the dead hand's mount, his right hand still clapped over his bleeding shoulder. He detoured to retrieve his Winchester, then ran the horse down, fighting off the wooziness as he climbed into the saddle.

Now it was a horse race.

17

ON the unfamiliar mount, Lex pushed after the fleeing cowhand. He knew he'd winged him, but there was no blood on the ground, and he didn't know how badly the man had been hit. As he rode, he ripped off his shirt sleeve and looked at his own wound. A deep furrow had been plowed across the outside of his left arm. The bullet hadn't struck any bone, but there was a lot of bleeding.

Lex bound the wound with the torn sleeve, wrapping it twice around and pulling it as tight as he could with his good hand and holding the other end of the wrapping with his teeth. Knotting the sleeve took three tries before he could keep it tight enough to hold the bleeding down.

There was some pain, but not enough to keep him from using the arm, if he had to. He could see the small puffs of dust in the flats kicked up by the fleeing man's horse. The cowhand was heading toward Carney. Lex had to hope he was also heading toward his boss. In the back of his mind was the conviction that the tall cowboy was central; if not the ringleader, then certainly close enough to it. If the wounded man was scared enough, he might lead Lex straight to the man who gave him his orders.

The light-headed feeling came and went. Sometimes the terrain seemed to swim underwater, and he'd shake his head to clear his vision. His body would adjust to the loss of blood, as long as he didn't lose any more. The strange horse seemed frightened of him, and Lex leaned forward to pat its neck and try to calm it down. It was a big chestnut stallion, and the horse had been well cared for. Unless he did something stupid, Lex knew he'd have no trouble hanging with his prey.

A meandering line of trees appeared on the horizon, and Lex recognized the creek that led past the back of Isaac Otterkill's place. He wondered for a moment if that's where the wounded man was going. It hadn't been Lucas or Daniel, he was sure of that. But maybe a friend. Maybe there was more truth to the accusations against Billy Otterkill than anyone thought.

When he reached the trees, Lex eased back and followed the creek eastward a few hundred yards. Somewhere along in here, he knew, the wounded man had made his passage. He was about to give it up and go on through himself when he found what he was looking for. A few leaves on a low-hanging willow branch glistened in the sunlight. When he looked closer, he saw they had been smeared with blood. The files swarming around were all the proof he needed that the blood was fresh.

Lex pushed on through. The water in the creek bottom was clear upstream, but looking downstream, he could see little clouds of mud. He pushed his borrowed mount downstream, keeping one eye straight ahead and the other on the roiled water. Through the clear stream, he could see an occasional hoofprint in the fine sand on the creek bottom.

The tracks angled toward the bank after about two hundred yards. He found another smear of blood on another willow branch, and he nudged the chestnut up the shallow bank and on into the brittle grass beyond the trees.

Far off across the flatlands, he could see the dark shape of the wounded man. It looked as if he were leaning badly, trying to hang onto the saddle, but coming close to losing his grip. It was still a few miles to town, but the gap was a long one.

Lex pushed his horse a little harder, trying to keep the man in sight, but the horse slowly sank below a gentle ridge line and the man was abruptly out of sight. Lex worried the man might be going for help. He was in no shape for another gun battle, not until he got some rest and had his arm tended to. But time was slipping away, and if he had to track the cowhand right to the mouth of the bear's den, then that's how it would have to be. No way in hell was he letting this one fish out of the net, not when there didn't seem to be another in sight.

When he reached the ridgeline himself, he found a dis

turbance in the dry ground. He reined in, knowing he was losing time, but not wanting to miss something significant. He knelt beside the strange markings. Smears of blood, a few drops and a couple of lumps of blood dirt told the story. The man had fallen, either completely off his mount or after having dismounted for some reason.

Lex could see where the horse had circled back, and where the wounded man had climbed back into the saddle, dragging one foot a few feet before managing to get his leg up and over the saddle. But the cowhand was still almost as far in the lead as he had been when he'd gone over the ridge.

Lex pushed harder now. He could see the roofs of the taller buildings in Carney, and he wanted to get to town as soon after his quarry as possible. He spotted a few drops of blood, but there was no indication the wounded man had fallen a second time.

He saw Elizabeth Helderson's boarding house off to the left. The tracks veered slightly, and Lex thought perhaps the man would head for the nearest house to get help, but the tracks seemed to straighten themselves out after fifty or sixty yards, as if the man had either changed his mind or regained control of a drifting mount.

The town began to take shape in the oppressive heat. The buildings shimmered, and the brilliant sun winked back at him from several windows as he rose and fell in the saddle. When he reached the edge of town, the tracks disappeared in a welter of hoofprints left by regular traffic. Lex pulled back on the reins and slowed his horse to a walk.

Blood was going to be the only lead now. He saw a couple of drops in the dust, then a couple more, small ones, as if the man had all but controlled the bleeding. Lex dismounted at the first hitching post. He stayed in the street, his Winchester crooked through his right arm, the hammer back. He was not going to take any chances. Watching every alley, he moved from horse to horse. He was nearly at the center of town by the time he found a bay with a bloody saddle.

The animal was hitched just to the right of the Flying Dutchman. Lex looked up the street, but there was no sign of blood in the dusty ruts. On the boardwalk in front of the saloon, he found two more stains, small drops. He reached down to brush them with his fingertips, and the sticky fluid smeared under his touch.

He found two more in the alley beside the saloon, and another on wooden stairs that led up the back to the second floor. Half a dozen rented rooms lined the back, and a wooden balcony ran the length of the building. Lex took the stairs carefully. He found one more smear of blood, this one on the banister at the top of the stairs, just before the landing, as if the wounded man had leaned on the splintered wood to catch his breath or take his bearings.

Lex moved on tiptoe. He listened at the first door, but heard no sound. The room might have been deserted. The second was occupied, judging by the sounds of rutting and the creaking of bed springs. He knew bar girls from the Flying Dutchman did more than serve drinks, and apparently one of them was earning an extra dollar or two. The man he wanted was in no shape to roll in the hay, so Lex moved on to the third door. This one sounded empty as well. He tried the knob and the door swung open. A thick cloud of cheap perfume drifted through the open door, and Lex shoved the door open wide. No one challenged him, and he ducked his head in. An empty bed, its spread neatly tucked in at the corners, suggested the room was empty.

Leaving the door open, he moved on to the fourth room. And the smear of blood on the doorframe told him all he needed to know. Lex leaned against the door, pressing his ear flat. At first, he heard nothing. Then footsteps cracked on the wood, found a carpet, then bare wood again.

He thought about knocking, but if the gunman was still inside, he didn't want to give any more warning than he could help. In all likelihood, there was a woman in there with him, who might or might not be involved in the rustling. Either way, Lex was not the kind to expose a woman to harm if he could avoid it. He backed toward the railing then measured the distance. Taking a half-step toward the door, he planted his foot squarely in the center panel.

The impact splintered the cheap latch free, and the door flew open with a loud bang that redoubled as it slammed into the wall. Lex waited a split second, then dove through the opening. A gun went off, but the shot went high and slammed into the wall several feet above him.

"Don't shoot," a woman shouted. Lex steeled himself, expecting a shriek, but he was off the mark.

A figure moved in the shadows in one corner of the room, and he realized it was a woman. She glided toward him on bare feet. He could see the white nightgown, turned gray by the shadow, then a brilliant white as the woman stopped in the block of light coming through the open door.

"You want to get me evicted?" she said, her voice husky, but not theatrically seductive. As his eyes adjusted to the contrasting light and darkness in the room, she came into focus.

Delilah.

She held a Colt revolver in her hand, barrel gripped comfortably in her long fingers, the butt extended toward Lex. "Take this thing," she said, "before somebody gets hurt. He's unconscious now."

"Who is he?"

"His name's Peter Johns."

"You don't have the best taste in friends, Delilah."

She looked at him strangely. "Good men have a funny habit around me. Either they look the other way, or they up and die."

"So you hang out with the likes of this bastard?"

"Hey, Cranshaw, you didn't seem interested. I've looked around pretty hard. You think Carney has a whole lot to offer a girl, especially a girl like me? I have my standards, too, you know."

She seemed to notice his wound for the first time. "You're hurt."

Lex shrugged. "I'll live."

"I'm not so sure about Pete. He the one who shot you?"

"One of 'em."

She nodded her head slowly. "He's the only one left, then, I guess."

"I wish. There were three other men who left before the shooting started. Three others weren't so lucky."

"And what did they do that was so horrible you had to shoot them?"

Lex debated for a moment. He didn't know what harm it would do to tell her, but on the other hand, he didn't know exactly where her loyalties, assuming she had any, might lie.

He decided to chance it. "I think they were the ones who killed Billy Otterkill."

She gasped then, and backed away. It wasn't the reaction he had expected. From the darkness, she said, "You better let me look at that arm. There's no doctor in Carney, but that shouldn't come as any big surprise. There's no church, either."

Lex laughed. "Something tells me neither one of us has much use for a church."

She didn't answer right away. It took him a moment to realize she was crying to herself. She stepped back into the light, a bowl of water, two towels, and a roll of gauze bandage in her hands. Two streams of tears wound down her cheeks. They sparkled when the sunlight hit them, and for a second it looked as if liquid fire was coursing down her face.

"What's wrong?" he asked.

"Nothing."

"Don't lie to me, Delilah. Everybody else in town has

tried that. I wish to Christ just one damn person around here would tell me the truth."

"About what?"

"About anything, damn it!"

Delilah didn't say anything immediately. She walked toward him, then tugged him toward a chair in the corner. She set the bowl and bandages on a small table beside the chair, leaned forward and pecked him on the lips, then, her palms flat against his chest, she pushed him into the chair. She knelt beside him and started working on the bloody knot in his sleeve.

She watched his arm closely while she worked. Finally, when the knot came free, she looked up into his face. "What do you want to know?" she asked.

"It's a long list."

"The days are long in Carney, Cranshaw. Always."

DELILAH looked at his arm, and Lex sat there, one eye riveted to the shadow on the bed, the other on the woman. He felt that the man was his key, but he was unconscious and there was no time to wait for him to regain consciousness. For a moment, he played with her name, rolling its music over and over in his mind, then wondered why.

She was so much prettier than he had thought. The big dark eyes, full of fire sometimes, and then when she withdrew, going cold and hard, were almost perfect. Her figure was fuller than he remembered, its shadowy contours alluring behind the thin cloth of the nightgown. Time and her work had not been all that kind to her, but there was still something in her that preserved the spark of a more innocent time. She felt his eyes on her and looked up, a smile tugging at the corners of her mouth.

"We better get that shirt off you," she said. She reached for the buttons and he tried to stop her, but she was insistent. As she peeled the shirt back, the notebook fell into his lap. And then he knew.

She looked at the book for a second, reached for it, and his hand closed over her wrist.

"Tell me about the letter you got from Billy," he said.

"What letter? I never got . . . "

"Don't lie to me, Delilah. Tell me about it."

She straightened then, and backed away from him. He started to get up, thinking she was going to run for the door, but she just moved to a small, battered vanity in the corner. Opening the single drawer in the ancient piece of furniture, she took out a small box, walked slowly back and set it in his lap.

"See for yourself," she said.

Lex opened the box. There was a small envelope, just like the other two he'd seen. This one was addressed to Deborah Murphy. He looked up and she smiled. "Delilah's more colorful, don't you think? That's important in my line of work."

Lex held the envelope for a moment, and Delilah, stamping her foot, snatched it out of his hands. She opened the envelope and took out three pages. He knew, even in the dim light, they were the pages from Billy Otterkill's notebook.

She opened the pages, smoothed them against her stomach, then started to read.

"Dear Lilah,

Something's going on here. I don't know what.

They are taking Mr. Holliman's cows and changing the brands. I have been watching them for three months and I don't know what to do. So far, they have changed the brand on nearly two hundred cows. To Paw's brand. If anything happens to me, tell Sheriff Harkness. Give him this letter.

Love,
Billy"

"This is what you want," she said, handing him the two remaining pages.

One was a simple map of the canyon, and the other contained the same numbers and dates Lex had seen in the notebook. Lex looked at her for a long time. "Did you show this to Harkness?"

"No . . . "

"Why in hell not?"

"Billy was already dead when it came. I didn't think there was any point."

"So you don't know who was stealing the cattle. Is that it?"

"I can guess."

"Guess, then . . . "

"Anse Mason's behind it."

"Why do you say that?"

"Because I've heard things. He talks in his sleep. Especially when he's been drinking. And he never comes here unless he's been drinking. He killed Billy. I'm sure of it."

"Why?"

"He hated Billy. Billy . . . " She turned away abruptly. moving toward the door, she passed through the bright sunlight for a second. Lex could see her shoulders shaking with silent sobbing. From across the room, she continued to speak, her voice shaking now, and broken by fits of sniffling sobs. "Billy stopped him from . . . Mason was . . . he . . . Mason attacked that girl, that Beatrice . . . you know how I mean . . . and Billy . . . Billy stopped him . . . Billy was . . . he hated Billy for that."

"And then Billy found out about the rustling so Mason decided to get even and cover his tracks at the same time . . . "

"I don't know. I guess . . . damn you, Cranshaw. I had it all under control."

It was all starting to fit together now. He could see Mason's face, the cancerous sneer as he jerked Delilah away from the table that night in the saloon.

"What else can you tell me? What else did Billy tell you?"

Delilah got up and backed away from him. She turned her back before she answered. "I don't know . . . I can't . . . nothing . . . "

"Delilah, you have to help me."

"Billy's dead. Nothing else matters."

"You're wrong. Five other men are dead. If you don't help me, Mason will get away with what he's already done, and maybe others will be killed. Maybe even you. Is that what you want?"

"I don't care. Don't you understand that? I don't care. This whole town should die. Every last self-righteous, hypocritical bastard in it should rot in hell. I just don't give a damn."

Lex took a deep breath. There had to be some way to shake loose whatever else she knew. And he was certain she knew more, maybe things she didn't even know were significant. But he had to be patient. He had to play her like a trout. If he wanted to land her, he couldn't afford a single mistake. Paying out line was as crucial as reeling it in. He changed tack.

"You and Billy. Tell me about that."

"There's nothing to tell."

"That's a load of horseshit, Delilah."

"It's none of your business."

"Who killed him is my business. And I know Anse Mason had something to do with it. You said as much yourself. I can't prove it though. I know he did it, but I need help. I need a witness. I need a reason. I need you to tell me what you know, damn it!"

"You don't give a damn about me, or about Billy."

Lex sighed. "Delilah, if Billy meant anything to you, then you should want the man who killed him to be punished."

"It won't bring Billy back."

"No, it won't."

"And what happens to me then? What kind of life do I have? What is there for me in Carney? And where can I go?"

Lex shook his head. She was so damn close to right that there was no point in trying to tell her otherwise. "Mason . . . tell me about him."

"There's nothing to tell. He's a bastard. All men are bastards. He's just bigger than most."

"You're afraid of him, aren't you?"

"Why shouldn't I be? Everybody else around here is afraid of him. Even Steve Holliman is afraid of him."

"I'm not afraid of him."

"Then kill him. Do the world a favor, Cranshaw. Go out there and kill him."

"I can't do that. Not unless he gives me a reason."

"He's breathing. Isn't that reason enough? You know he killed Billy. Isn't that reason enough? He killed those others. He killed the sheriff. Aren't those reasons enough? How many reasons do you need, for God's sake?"

"But I need proof."

She shook her head. "No, you don't. He did it and you know it. Just tell him. See what he does."

"You want him to get himself killed. You want me to shoot him because you can't deal with the truth. If Anse Mason goes under the ground, you think that will solve your problems. But it won't."

She laughed. The sound was cold and bitter in the small, gloomy room. "What problems, Cranshaw? I don't have any problems."

"I don't have time for this, Delilah. I can't be a minister for you. I'm a lawman. You want something from me I can't give you. You want what other folks get from church. You want to go to church and pray, you do that. But don't ask me to go with you."

"Church. Cranshaw, look around you. You think I'm the kind of girl who goes to church?"

"Once upon a time, probably."

"You bastard . . ."

Lex ignored her now. He took a towel and soaked it in the bowl on the table and started to clean his wounded arm. The water stung and he gritted his teeth. He took a second towel and mopped at the bloody mess, then took the gauze and unrolled a couple of feet. Delilah walked toward him, her steps hesitant, but he waited. She reached out for the bandage and knelt beside him.

"Let me do that," she said.

She took the gauze and wrapped it carefully, making sure the bandage stayed flat. He held his arm out to make her task easier. Gritting his teeth as she tightened the bandage, he groaned involuntarily. She wrapped the last few inches, then made a neat, flat knot. "That's the best I can do," she said.

"Thank you." He reached for his shirt but she grabbed it away. "You can't wear that. I have something better." She disappeared into the shadows again and was back a moment later with a clean shirt.

He tried it on. It was a little snug, but it would do.

"That was Billy's," she said.

He nodded. "Mason didn't like you seeing Billy, did he?"

Delilah didn't answer right away. Lex let the question hang in the air, knowing he'd hooked her securely, at last.

When she finally spoke, it was with the voice of a much older woman, a woman who has seen the end of her life from close range and was too weary to back away from it. "No, he didn't. He killed the first two, Simmons and Berger, because they were getting cold feet. He talks a lot when he comes here. He's usually drunk, and . . . anyway. They were getting cold feet. They threatened to tell Steve Holliman what was going on."

"So he killed them . . . "

She nodded. "Then, when Billy told me he saw Mason in that canyon a couple of days before Holliman found his cows there, I . . . Look, I never thought anything would happen to Billy. I told him to forget what he saw. There was no place to go anyway. Harkness was scared of Mason. And then Mason offered him a cut."

She droned on for several minutes, her voice flat and almost funereal. It all came pouring out of her in a continuous monotone. When she was done, he had all the pieces. And they all fit. Delilah lay her head in his lap. Lex stroked her hair, trying to comfort her and knowing it was beyond him.

"You'll testify?" he asked.

Delilah nodded. "Yes." She got up then, and walked toward the open doorway. She turned to face him, the bright light making her look older than her years. Her eyes were red and her lips trembled. But she said nothing more.

Lex got up and walked toward her. "You'll be all right?"

She nodded again. "I'll be all right, yes."

Lex walked out onto the balcony and started toward the stairs. When he started down, she called after him, "Cranshaw?"

He turned.

"You be careful."

19

THE Holliman ranch was about as far from Carney as money could manage. Eight miles north of town, it sat in a pleasant valley. There was plenty of water from a fork of the Pecos River, and the sweeping reaches of tall grass looked about as unlike the rest of the territory as Lex could imagine. Steve Holliman had cornered the only decent water for fifty miles in any direction.

The house itself was huge. Three stories tall, painted in blinding white that reflected the brilliant sun, the house reminded Lex of those plantation houses that dotted so much of the south. But unlike those he'd seen in Georgia and Mississippi during the war, this one had its best days ahead of it. From its location on a gentle rise, it dominated the valley on all sides.

The road led down through the grass, then through

a gate in a split-rail fence nearly half-a-mile away from the front porch. The outbuildings were spanking new, the barn sporting a fresh coat of deep red paint, the others, including a bunkhouse and a couple of other low-lying structures Lex couldn't identify, wore recent whitewash. They didn't sparkle quite as brilliantly as the main house, but then such buildings were meant to support it, not steal its thunder.

The gate was open. Lex rode through it, under a raw timber arch from which dangled a broad walnut plank bearing the Holliman brand, an *L* lying on its side. Lex glanced up at the brand as he rode under it, thinking how easy it had been to change the brand to Isaac Otterkill's Rocking U. He hadn't seen a soul yet, but there were a dozen horses in a corral alongside the barn, two dozen more in a larger pen behind the bunkhouse.

As he rode into the front yard, Lex felt his gut clench, and the tension tightened the muscles across his back and shoulders. His wounded arm began to throb a little, and he could see a small bloodstain on the sleeve of his borrowed shirt. He closed his hand over the wound for a second, squeezing it until the pain subsided.

He dismounted halfway across the yard and walked his horse to the elaborate hitching post off to one end of the columned porch. A tall, thin black man in black pants and an immaculate white jacket stepped through the open French doors onto the porch as Lex approached the steps.

Lex stopped with one foot on the first step. The black man watched him curiously, but said nothing.

"Mr. Holliman to home?" Lex asked.

"Yes, sir." The butler's eyes lingered on his gunbelt for a moment, then drifted up to scrutinize the ranger's face. "Who shall I say is calling?"

"Lex Cranshaw."

"Mr. Holliman is expecting you, sir?"

"No, I don't think so."

"Please wait inside." The butler turned and stepped back through the broad doorway, then waited for Lex to join him. The interior of the house was even more impressive. Thick carpets covered gleaming hardwood floors. The high ceilings were elaborately ornamented with thick mouldings and gold inlay. Beyond the foyer, a hallway ran straight through the center of the house, leading to a matching pair of French doors at the other end. Those doors, too, were open, giving a panoramic view of the valley and the ridge beyond it.

This was money, big money, Texas-sized money. And Holliman would almost certainly have an ego to match his bank account. Lex had yet to meet a man who had enough money to buy God a present, who didn't also have enough pride to give Satan a run for his money.

The butler disappeared halfway down the hall. Lex stood with his back to the front doors, his hands clasped behind his back. The butler returned a minute later, came halfway back to meet Lex, and said, "Mr. Holliman will see you now."

He retreated toward the same doorway through which he'd disappeared a moment before, and waited for Lex to catch up. Then he stepped into a huge room that

must have been Holliman's office and library. Lex was
conscious of his dirty boots on a thick carpet whose rich
colors seemed even brighter under the dusty leather.
Bookshelves from ceiling to floor occupied one whole
wall. An oak ladder on a metal track ran up nearly to
the ceiling to give access to the books on the higher
shelves.

Dead center, a desk as big as the Cranshaw dining-
room table back in Kentucky, its wood gleaming as if it
emitted light from somewhere deep inside the walnut, hid
the lower half of the man who owned everything he could
see from his front porch, and more than a little beyond.

He was expensively dressed, and as he stood to step
out from behind the desk, his hand-tooled Mexican boots
squeaked the way only new leather can. He was a big
man, probably six feet or a little over, and when he took
Lex's hand, the ranger could feel the man's physical
power. The grip was firm and seemed genuine.

"Mr. Cranshaw, I've been wondering when you would
get around to seeing me."

"It hasn't been all that quiet since I've been here," Lex
said.

"Would you care for some whiskey? I have some Jim
Beam. An excellent bourbon, if you've never tried it."

"I'm from Lexington, Kentucky, originally."

"Then you are aware of Mr. Beam and his product."

Lex nodded. "Thank you. I wouldn't mind a drink."

"Water?"

"Please."

Holliman busied himself with the bourbon and poured

water from a crystal decanter into a pair of small glasses, handed one to Lex and took a sip of his own before returning to the high-backed leather chair behind his desk. As he sat down, he indicated another chair, also covered in leather, to one side. "Have a seat, Mr. Cranshaw."

When Lex sat down, Holliman cleared his throat. "Now, what can I do for you, Mr. Cranshaw?"

"I'd like to ask you a few questions, if I might."

"Feel free."

"I understand you've been losing quite a few cattle in the last six months."

"That's true, yes."

"You have any idea who's responsible?"

"None."

"How about the sheriff?"

"Sheriff Harkness is dead. I'm sure you are aware of that."

"But did he have any idea who was responsible?"

"Not that I know of."

"He didn't tell you he thought Billy Otterkill was behind it?"

"No."

"Did you have any reason to suspect Billy Otterkill?"

"Not really."

Lex chewed that cabbage a bit, leaning back in his chair and taking a sip of the bourbon. He rubbed one hand across his chin, listening to the rasp of skin on whiskers. He twiddled with his mustache a moment, took another sip, then leaned forward.

"What do you know about Anse Mason?"

Holliman shrugged. "As much as I need to. He's been my foreman for three years. He's a good worker. A little bit of a bully, I guess. At least, he pushes the men hard, too hard, sometimes. But I have no complaints."

"Would it surprise you if I told you I have reason to believe Mason is the man behind the rustling?"

"Yes, it would." It was Holliman's turn to mull things over. He ran a nervous hand through his thick black hair, then smoothed his sideburns back into place. "Very much."

"Is he around?"

"Should be in the bunkhouse."

"Mind if I have a few words with him?"

"You're wasting your time, but, no, I don't mind. I'll have Jason get him." He stood and walked toward the office door. "Jason?"

"Mr. Holliman?"　.

"You mind getting Anse Mason over here?" Holliman glanced at Cranshaw. "And Jason, don't tell him Mr. Cranshaw is here. Just tell him I want to speak to him a moment."

"Yes, sir." The butler vanished down the hall, and Lex heard his footsteps on the porch stairs.

"You say you have reason to suspect Mason. You mind if I ask you what that reason is?"

"I'd rather wait until he's here, Mr. Holliman. No point in running through it twice."

Holliman nodded. "All right."

"You happen to know whether Mason owns a buffalo gun, by any chance?"

"As a matter of fact, I think . . . " Footsteps on the porch interrupted him. He fell silent and waited with his hands fidgeting on the desktop.

Lex reached down and loosened the Colt in his holster. Holliman noticed and raised an eyebrow, but he didn't comment.

A moment later, a large figure filled the doorframe. Anse Mason was even bigger than Lex remembered. And the first glimpse clicked home. Mason was the tall cowhand from the canyon. There was no doubt about it. Every last piece was available now. All Lex had to do was lay the puzzle on the table and put it together.

"You wanted to see me, Mr. Holliman?" Mason said. He glared at Lex, but made no show of courtesy.

"Mr. Cranshaw wants to ask you a few questions. You mind?"

"Long as I don't have to like it."

"You *won't* like it, Anse. I can promise you that." Lex stood up. He didn't want to be too comfortable in the cushioned chair. "Where were you yesterday morning, Mason?" he began.

"Working. Like I am every damn day this time of year. Late summer roundup." He glanced at Holliman, maybe for support, maybe for an inkling as to where this was leading. Lex watched the rancher at the same time. He noticed a certain glimmer in the man's eyes. Maybe fear, he thought. But of what?

"You weren't running some of Mr. Holliman's cattle down past Sulfur Valley were you, by any chance? A little box canyon?"

"Hell, no, I wasn't. What are you trying to suggest?"

"I'm not suggesting anything, Mason. I'm telling you. I was there. I saw you."

"Must be mistaken, Cranshaw."

"You killed Billy Otterkill, didn't you."

"Bastard deserved what he got, but no, I didn't have nothing to do with that."

"And I suppose you didn't hang Simmons and Berger, either."

"Now why would I do something like that?"

"Because they were going to tell your boss exactly what you were doing with his property."

"Who told you that . . . that's bullshit, Cranshaw." But he was off balance now, and Holliman leaned forward, a curious look on his face.

Lex bored in harder. "You killed Billy, but you didn't know he kept records." Lex reached into his shirt for Billy's notebook. He brought it out and tapped it on outstretched fingers. "It's all here. Chapter and verse, Mason, all of it. And I have a witness. You want me to read the dates to you? And the number of cattle on each of those dates? You want me to tell Mr. Holliman why you hanged the sheriff, and how you killed those other two men, trying to pin it on Isaac Otterkill?" Lex stopped to let it sink in. "Or do *you* want to tell him?"

"I don't have to listen to this shit!" He backed through the door and broke into a run.

LEX sprinted after Mason, nearly knocking Jason over as he barreled into the hallway. The butler pointed and Lex charged toward the French doors at the rear of the house. He skidded to a halt on a broad stone patio. Instinctively, he dropped into a crouch, scanning the rear yard for a glimpse of the fleeing foreman.

He saw Mason then, running flat-out toward the bunkhouse. Lex called to him to halt, but Mason ignored him. Lex leaped off the patio and landed in full stride. He chased after the foreman, expecting him to run into the bunkhouse, but Mason veered to the left. Without breaking stride, he vaulted over a low fence and hauled himself up and over a corral fence beyond. Lex fired into the air once, but the gunshot seemed only to galvanize the fugitive.

Horses scattered left and right, one rising up on its hind legs and clawing at the sky. He saw Mason climbing the opposite fence then, and as Lex leaped over the low fence beside the bunkhouse, he caught a glimpse of several horses on the far side of the corral, all saddled.

Mason was mounted as Lex stopped at the corral fence. Turning back toward the house, he ran for his own mount. Mason fired twice, the shots kicking up clods of dirt a few yards ahead of Lex and to the left.

He unknotted the reins and climbed into the saddle, jerking the horse around so viciously the animal shook its head in rage trying to shake off the demon on its back. Digging his spurs into the chestnut's flanks, he raced toward the bunkhouse. The direct route ran through the corral, but there was no way Lex was going to jump the fence into the milling horses. Sawing on the reins, he cut right, racing past the bunkhouse as half a dozen men spilled out into the sunlight.

"What the hell's going on?" one of them shouted. He carried a rifle and waved it at Lex, but the ranger dashed past and turned the corner of the bunkhouse. He could see Mason across the valley floor. He had a good mount, and the man was running for his life. The thick grass cushioned the thunder of hooves, reducing the sound to the beating of an enormous heart.

Lex pulled his Colt and fired once, but Mason was too far away. He reholstered the pistol and ducked low in the saddle, trying to cut down the wind resistance. Mason was a good horseman, and he knew the terrain. He was heading toward the Pecos Fork, and Lex saw the sunlight glint off the spray kicked up by Mason's horse as the animal plunged into the broad, shallow branch.

He was two-thirds of the way across, losing ground now, but still out of pistol range. Lex closed fast, hoping to reach the river before Mason climbed the far bank, but he still had two hundred yards to go as Mason's mount broke out of the river and lunged up the bank.

Plunging into the river, the chestnut struggled against the water and the uncertain footing beneath it. The animal tried to keep up its speed, but the river was too much for it. As the water came up past the stirrups, the horse slowed to a walk, and Lex watched helplessly as Mason charged up the deep green of the ridge, putting more and more distance between him and his pursuer.

Lex backed off the spurs, letting the chestnut find its own pace. By the time they regained shallow water on the far side, Mason was nearly to the ridgeline at the top of the valley. Lex pushed his mount again, and the chestnut struggled up the bank, losing its footing once, then regaining it and digging in as its hind legs cleared the bank.

Lex charged up the ridge as Mason reached the top and cut to his left. The foreman ran parallel to the crest for a hundred yards, then slowly drifted out of sight on the far side as Lex barreled straight uphill. Free of the river's resistance, the chestnut had settled into an effortless gallop. Lex rode easily, only dimly conscious of the throbbing in his left arm.

As he reached the crest of the ridge, he looked back toward the river. Half a dozen mounted men, at least two of them in undershirts, galloped toward the river. He didn't know whether they were coming to his assistance or to Mason's but there was no time to worry about it.

On top of the ridge, he looked out at the broad arid valley ahead. The terrain seemed to grow progressively more barren as it receded into the distance. Nudging the horse over and down, he cut at an angle across the face of the ridge, trying to give his mount a less breakneck descent.

Mason was already on the valley floor, his horse kicking up a swirling trail of dust that corckscrewed across the flats, then trailed away into thin air a couple of hundred feet behind the animal. Mason had a big lead, and Lex thought about reining in and using his rifle, but at that range, he was stretching the limits of marksmanship, and Mason was already far ahead. Any more, and it might not be possible to catch him. Lex was not interested in spending the next couple of days tracking a desperate man with a Sharps in his saddle boot.

Far to the left, another cloud of dust, this one larger than that Mason was leaving behind, angled across the valley floor. If Mason saw it, he paid no attention, neither veering toward it nor angling away. As the ridge began to flatten out toward the valley floor, Lex pushed the chestnut still harder, and the animal responded with a burst of speed as it hit the level ground.

Lex was only halfway across the broad floor of the valley when Mason started up the next ridge. The sun was still high in the sky, and Lex glanced up at it for a second, trying to gauge the time left before sundown. At least four hours, he figured, maybe a little more. It was a long time, but was it enough, he wondered.

The cloud across the valley was changing direction now, veering toward Mason's tail, but it was further away than Lex was. And in the back of the ranger's mind was that buffalo gun. If Mason wasn't too scared, he just might choose to make a stand on the high ground. The Sharps could keep Lex at arm's length until nightfall, leaving Mason free to make his escape in the dark.

Reaching the first gentle hint of the ascent, Lex slowed to watch Mason, now almost on top of the ridge. The foreman reined in suddenly and Lex saw him slide from the saddle and yank a rifle from the saddle boot. The foreman waved his hat at the horse, then ran across the ridgeline toward a pile of broken rocks.

There was no cover down below, and Lex cut to the left, trying to give Mason as tough a target as possible. With any luck, he'd be able to cut back and angle across the face again, closing the gap, if he could keep Mason off balance.

But the first thunderclap from the Sharps changed all that. The chestnut missed a step, then a second. It staggered, trying to keep its feet, then went down on its knees, throwing Lex from the saddle. As he rolled over and scrambled to his feet, he looked back at the horse, trying to get up, but unable to. It was bleeding heavily from a bullet wound in the neck, through and through. Its frantic breath bubbled in its throat, and blood burbled through both bullet holes as it sank down and rolled onto its side.

Lex looked up in time to see Mason complete a triumphant wave of his fist, then race toward his horse. There was more gunfire now, but not from Mason. Off to the left, the cloud had resolved itself into three horsemen. They were all firing rifles from horseback. As Lex looked back toward Mason's cover, he saw the foreman's horse, a hundred yards closer to the mounted men. Puffs of dust were kicking up around it as the horsemen charged closer, concentrating their fire on the mount. It would take a lucky shot, but the horse was a hell of a lot bigger target than Mason himself.

Lex scrambled toward his own dying mount and yanked his Winchester free, thankful the horse hadn't buried it under him. He used the chestnut for cover. The great flanks throbbed and the bubbling breathing grew more sporadic. Lex yanked his Colt and put the animal out of its misery.

Another booming shot from the Sharps echoed across the valley, and the heavy buffalo slug slammed into the horse and burst through just inches from Lex's head.

The buffalo gun was a single shot rifle, and in the time it took Mason to reload, Lex zigzagged up the slope toward a flat slab of red rock. It wasn't very thick, but it canted up the slope and would cover him if he lay flat. He dove to the ground then wormed up close to the rock, his chest heaving and his wounded arm throbbing more painfully.

The Sharps cracked again, but there was no sound from the bullet either whistling by overhead or slamming into the ground around him. Lex peeked up and saw one of the three horsemen leap from his stumbling mount as the other two charged on.

At almost the same moment, out of the corner of his eye, he saw Mason's horse jump, then fall to its knees. The animal had been hit, maybe not badly, but badly enough to make it useless to Mason. Lex clambered over the flat rock and headed for the next cover, twenty yards uphill. The next rock was smaller, but still large enough to conceal him.

The two horsemen charged on, one firing at Mason to try and keep him honest while the other emptied his magazine in the direction of Mason's wounded horse. They broke off suddenly, and came charging downhill toward Lex.

Out of the corner of his eye, Lex saw Mason get to one knee and draw a bead with the big buffalo gun. Swinging the Winchester up, he aimed a little high to allow for the bullet's drop as it ran out of steam. He was rewarded with chips of rock from the boulder hiding Mason's lower half, and the foreman ducked down involuntarily. The Sharps went off anyway, but the shot was way off the mark and sailed harmlessly past the horsemen.

Lex got to his feet and charged another ten feet uphill. There were plenty of rocks to choose from, but most of them were too small to offer him full cover, and they slowed him down as he zigzagged across the face of the hill.

The two horsemen jumped from their mounts, and raced toward Lex on foot. With a shock, he recognized Isaac Otterkill, falling a little behind his younger son as they dashed across the rocky hill. Lucas turned to look uphill at Mason, then spun and grabbed his father, pulling him to the ground as the Sharps went off again.

Isaac went down and scrambled in behind a jumble of small boulders. Lucas dropped to his knees, fishing in his pocket for ammunition and slipped shell after shell into the magazine loader of his Winchester. Lex fired twice more to give the kid time to finish.

Isaac nodded toward Lex, but said nothing. They had Mason pinned now. They were close enough that the Sharps was no longer an advantage. Smoking him out was not going to be easy, but at least they didn't have to worry about him breaking away.

Shouts from far below snapped Lex around, and he saw the half-dozen Lazy L riders from Holliman's ranch charging up the slope far behind him.

Lex lay flat on the ground and crept to one edge of the rock, cupping his hands around his mouth. "Give it up, Mason."

The Sharps barked, and the slug fractured on Lex's cover, while its echo rolled downhill like a clap of thunder.

Lucas was done reloading and was working on his father's rifle now. Lex waited for the kid to finish. Far across the slope, Daniel Otterkill raced from rock to rock, but he was no threat to Mason, who ignored him. When both rifles were reloaded, Lucas glanced toward Lex.

"How in the hell did you happen to be here?" Lex asked.

Lucas grinned balefully. "We was watching you all

along. Soon's you left Delilah, we paid her a visit. She told us where you was headed. Figured you might need some help."

"Reckon I do."

"What shall we do?" Lucas asked.

"Cover me . . ."

"You sure?"

Lex nodded. He waited for the Otterkills to get ready, then raised a hand. They fired alternately, waiting for Mason to show himself before each shot, and Lex climbed to his feet and broke to the right. He zigged back to the left, his eyes riveted on Mason's cover. Everytime a flash of color showed the foreman was trying to draw a bead, a crack exploded downhill, and a bullet slammed into the top of the rock. Lex was closing the gap quickly now.

Less than thirty yards below the ridgeline, he ducked down behind a blocky stone. The Otterkills needed time to reload. When Lucas flashed the sign that they were ready, Lex turned and shouted, "Mason, give it up. You can't get out of this."

"Go to hell." The Sharps barked once more, a blind shot that sailed off into the valley.

Lex gave Lucas the high sign and broke from cover. As he charged the last few yards, Mason, desperate to reload the big buffalo gun, got to his feet, ignoring the guns below. He brought the Sharps around, but Lex was on him and launched himself over the top, his bad arm knocking the buffalo gun to one side. It flew from Mason's grasp as Lex barreled into him, knocking both men to the ground.

Mason was a lot bigger than Lex, and shoved his smaller adversary off him and rolled to one side. The men below couldn't risk a shot now. Mason backed away a step as Lex got up. He reached for his sidearm as Lex straightened.

Mason was fast, and the gun came up more quickly than Lex had expected. His own pistol was already in his fist as he dropped to his knees and squeezed the trigger. Mason's shot whistled past Lex's ear as Lex fired again. Two bright red flowers suddenly blossomed dead center on Mason's blue shirt. He staggered back, fell heavily and lay there gasping for breath.

Behind him, Lex heard Lucas Otterkill charging uphill. He turned to the kid. "It's over," he said.

Lucas ignored him. "Not yet, it ain't."

Isaac stepped past Lex, his thumb on his rifle's hammer. Before Lex could stop him, he shoved the Winchester into Mason's right eye and pulled the trigger.

Lucas stood there staring down at the bloody mess that had been Mason's head as Isaac turned to Lex.

The old man stuck his jaw out a bit, waiting for Lex to say something. But Lex just shook his head and Isaac smiled. "*Now* it's over," he said.

Dan Mason is the pseudonym of a full-time writer who lives in upstate New York with his family.